STUDIO CITY SONGS

ZAIDE WILLIAMS

CONTENTS

INTRODUCTION

This book has a musical backbeat, and you'll find many wonderful songs referenced within its pages. I'd love for you to check out the full *Studio City Songs* playlist on Spotify and groove along while you read.

Search for *Studio City Songs* on Spotify or simply click here and let the music play.

Z.W.

DROP THE NEEDLE

Your face is my star,
    Your laugh lights my sky
    I'd give the damn universe
    To get lost in your eyes.

I'll sing it
    I'll scream it
    But you gotta hear me say...

Take the world, darlin'
    Take the moon, baby
    Take everything I am
    Just please stay.

From "Take the Moon," music by Tiyani Keith and Gene Coltrane, lyrics by Gene Coltrane

PART I

COME TOGETHER

1
———

THE WAY YOU LOOK TONIGHT

June 1997
Nassau, Bahamas

"Don't touch there!"

"Glen, it's your forearm."

"But it huuuuurts!"

"That's because you fell asleep. Especially if you're a pasty British person who likes rain, you don't fall asleep at the beach on an eighty-five-degree day."

"I'm a Scot."

"My apologies, but still. Let me see. Oh, Glen. Did you put aloe on it?"

"I have, but it all oozed under the surface instantaneously, as though my skin were the Sahara." She tutted softly, pulling down the sleeve of her blouse. "But never mind that. Tell me—have the metaphorical hairpins come out yet?"

Munie just laughed and shook her head. Relaxing didn't come easy for her, especially these days. "The ones related to grad school, the ones related to Michael, or the ones related to Dad?"

"Take your pick."

She sighed, gazing around the open-air coffee shop, then moved her focus back across the bistro table to Glenys and shrugged. "Grad school, yes. I mean, I'm done—I graduated—so there's a check in that box."

"Right. And bravo again."

"Thanks. The other two are a little more convoluted."

"Also right." Glenys stood up, stretched, and grabbed an enormous sunhat. "Let's have a stroll, shall we? Might help to goose the thought process a bit."

The early evening streets of Nassau were as crammed as usual with tourists, street vendors, plastic signs and noise, but it was a warm and breezy evening and the night was young. Munie let her eyes pass over one unique spectacle after another, taking it all in. Modern, chic buildings mingled with dated, European-inspired architecture and colorful Caribbean tones. Art was everywhere she looked. On one corner, a cluster of local teens danced to a pop song on a boombox. Across the way, an artisan hawked hand-whittled wood carvings.

Even the buildings themselves held artistry. She was so mesmerized with the mural of a fruiting mango tree painted on the side of an old book shop that she almost smacked right into a group of (obvious) American tourists in front of her—T-shirt and ball cap-clad, talking too loudly and arguing with each other about what was on their paper street map. Across the street, a shirtless man with a long white beard regarded them with a small smile as he fed bits of melon to the parrot on his shoulder.

Glenys weaved her arm carefully through Munie's as they walked. "Which topic shall we address next? João the twat, perhaps?"

"My father is not a twat, although I do love the way you say that word."

"Well OK, then he's a pseudo-twat. Anyone who doesn't approve of you taking up a field like journalism is at minimum a pseudo-twat, possibly also bordering on asshat, but that title is still under discussion."

Munie squeezed her friend's arm gratefully.

"Ow!"

"Oh sorry!" She unhanded Glenys' forearm with an apologetic smile and patted her hand instead. "I'm just glad I have you in my corner."

"Always. And for piss sakes, you're a fully-grown adult. It's time for João to let you be and carry on with his middle-age crisis. Are we agreed on that point?"

It was easier to say than to manifest, but Glenys was right. "Yes, we're agreed," she answered with a sigh.

"Shall we move on to Michael, then?"

Munie snorted. "Ugh no. I have no bandwidth for fiancé drama right now."

"Fair enough, love. We'll classify that as a dilemma for another day."

They strolled for another few minutes in amiable silence, listening to the cacophony of the old town, smelling the sea air sprinkled with the sumptuous notes of food cooking on an outdoor grill nearby, and feeling the gentle caress of the evening breeze against their skin. Step by step, one by one, the hairpins continued to fall.

At length, they passed a classy-looking restaurant with a chalkboard sign at the front door:

Jazz Night

Esai Martinez & Company

6 & 9 PM

"Ooooh Glen—jazz! Let's go in. It starts in twenty minutes."

"Sounds lovely! It's your graduation party after all, ducks. And perhaps you can write about the performance afterward. Put that brand new Master's degree to use."

"Ha! I doubt it. And don't forget, we're also celebrating our birthdays."

"Correction—we're celebrating *my* birthday. You must wait until September to turn twenty-seven and experience all the wisdom afforded by this milestone."

Munie just laughed. "A mere technicality, and all the more reason to go to Madrid in the fall."

"Too right! Shall we, then?" Glenys opened the door with a flourish.

"Absolutely. Let's go."

It was one of those venues that Munie loved—an intimate supper club with small, round tables facing a close-up stage. Low lights, velvet drapes, and some well-placed rat-packery thrown in here and there for good measure made it feel like a little musical cocoon.

"Perfect," she cooed, taking her seat.

And true to any good night club, a server was swift to take their order and even swifter in whisking back over with a glass of red for Munie and a glass of white for Glenys.

"To music," Glenys offered with a wide smile, raising her sauvignon blanc in the air.

Twenty-five minutes later, as they were approaching the bottoms of their glasses, a collection of tuxedo-clad men walked onstage and took up their instruments. There was a drummer, a bass player, a pianist, a guitarist, and a full horn section, with a set of conga drums and timbales off to the side for good measure. The stage was chockfull of potential.

Munie mentally rubbed her hands together in anticipation. This was her passion, after all—feeling the energy and the beauty of live music, letting it infiltrate and nourish her every cell. Regardless of genre or venue, the experience always reached her deeply, leaving her somehow more vibrant, more connected, than she had been before the music started. If instinct served her right, tonight's dose of musical medicine would be an especially good one.

And boy, oh boy, it was. From the first full-on blast of sound, the place was on fire, vibrating with the joyful tones of well-executed Latin jazz. If she had to guess, she would have said the older man now at the timbales was Esai, the bandleader. But it was a kid playing sax who caught her attention from his first solo. He was fantastic—smooth and seasoned and wielding a musicality that stood out in clear silhouette even against this backdrop of excellent musicians.

She just kept watching him play, more impressed by the minute. Then he took a turn at the conga drums, burning up percussion on the classic 'Quimbara.' Then he was rocking at the piano. But it wasn't until the tail end of the show, when he stepped up to the mike to offer the only non-Latin jazz standard of the night, a delicate rendition of "The Way You Look Tonight" that Glenys echoed out loud precisely what was circling around the forefront of Munie's brain. "That young man is bloody brilliant."

The sound that came out of his mouth when he started to sing didn't fit the teenage boy from which it came. It was silky and multi-layered, smooth and textured all at once. She tried to make a comparison—Sam Cooke? Nat King Cole? None were enough. Whatever it was, it was one hundred percent old soul, and she was floored by it. And what he had by the multitude in talent wasn't lacking in charisma, she noted, watching him glide from one side of the floor to the other, gesturing along with the lyrics, from time to time sending a disarmingly dimpled grin into the audience. He was quite simply a star in the making.

"Munie love, I must say that was one of your better ideas. However, I need more aloe."

The show had just ended, and the crowd was beginning to disperse around the two friends as they polished off the shared slice of key lime pie that had gone wholly unnoticed during the performance.

"And I need a nap," Munie confessed. The heat, her full belly, and the previous week's finals schedule were creeping up on her slowly but surely, and her cozy ocean-front hotel bed was beckoning. "Want me to call the cab?"

"I've got it," Glenys replied, standing and stretching. "Ooh!" she called suddenly, looking toward the side of the room. "The band is there! Let's say hello."

"Glennnnn..."

"Just five minutes. I must tell them how delightful they were. Would that all right? No longer, I promise."

Although Munie would normally be completely gung-ho for a musical meet and greet, her glass of red was weighing heavily after a day in the sun, and she wasn't sure she'd be up to making sparkling conversation. Even so, she knew that not saying yes would be an opportunity missed. Her assent was more of a yawny groan than a verbal approval, but apparently it was enough for Glenys, who bee-lined it to join a short receiving line of audience members offering congratulations to Esai Martinez and his band.

The two friends made their way from front to back, starting with handsome, salt-and-pepper charming Esai and working down the single file of musicians, shaking hands and making conversation with everyone. Glenys was nothing but effusive when she got to the end of the line.

"Young man, you were spectacular!" she bubbled, taking his hand in both of hers. "What is your name?"

He smiled shyly at her unbridled exuberance. "Jackson Martinez Flores, ma'am." He had a beautiful smile.

"How old are you, may I ask?"

Oh, Glenys.

He just smiled again as if this was not at all the first time he'd heard that particular question. "I just turned seventeen, ma'am."

"Well my goodness, Jackson, you are a rare talent, indeed."

"Thank you, ma'am."

"I look forward to seeing you in all the magazines a few years from now. You know, my friend here is a journalist specializing in music. Perhaps she'll write about you one day, hey?"

He glanced toward Munie with a wide, disarming smile. "I look forward to being written about."

And he was witty to boot. Munie was becoming more impressed by the minute. This kid was the real deal.

"Munie, love, I'm going to powder my nose, then pop out to call us a taxi, yeah? Meet me out front?"

"Try the back exit," Jackson offered. "It's a lot faster this time of night. Safe too—lots of folks from here leave that way, so you won't be alone."

"Brilliant, dear, thank you. Mun—see you back there in a few?"

"Sure."

"Lovely to have met you, Jackson. All the best, lad."

"Pleasure," he replied, shaking Glenys' hand.

Jackson turned to Munie, that charming smile as bright as ever as he extended his arm to her. "May I walk you out?" She accepted with a nod and a little smile of her own, and began to slowly stroll with him toward the back of the venue.

"How long have you been playing?"

"Mmmmm, since I was about three maybe?"

"Three years old??"

"Yeah. Mom is an opera singer and plays the piano, so she started me off on that real early." Even at seventeen, he had an easy stride about him, like he was one hundred percent comfortable in his body —a rare thing in a teenager.

"And when did you pick up the sax? And percussion? And... all of it!?" She laughed and he returned her goodwill with a shy, self-deprecating smile.

"Just over time. My dad taught me everything."

"Wow. How long have you been with his band, then?"

His smile faded. "Oh, that's my Uncle Esai. My dad travels a lot. He's on the road now." Jackson looked down for just a second, and in that second Munie read volumes about the idolization of the father by the son and the isolation of the son by the father, for it was plain as day in the young man's change of energy and expression. Although Munie was good at reading people, in this case it was especially easy, for Jackson's visage was one she'd worn on her own face and heart more than once. She knew viscerally how low he must be feeling, so she pivoted.

"I don't play any instruments," she offered, her tone light. "I tried a bunch of times, but it's just not my thing."

He brightened. "Oh yeah? What'd you try?"

She chuckled to herself and shook her head, giving him a rueful sideways glance. "Flute, cello, and oboe."

"Oboe?! Why oboe?"

"Apparently it's supposed to be one of the most difficult instruments to play. My folks thought it would be a 'fitting challenge.'"

"Dang."

"Yeah. And nothing ever really clicked after that. I mean, I love music, but I've never been able to play it."

He stopped suddenly and turned to her. "Maybe you should have tried drums first."

"Why is that?"

He thought for a moment, running a hand down his mouth as he searched for the right words. "It's just ... the realest. Like the earth, like the elements."

"How so?"

Jackson grinned ear to ear as an idea struck him, dimples decorating both sides of his face. "Come here." He beckoned with a tilt of his head back toward the stage, then spun around and began walking.

"I can't!" Munie giggled as he stepped behind the conga drums and invited her to join him with a playful crook of his index finger. *Little devil*, she thought.

"Why not? Look, nobody's around. Just for a second."

Munie sighed and walked toward the stage, standing next to him as he placed one hand on each drum.

"Part of it is the tone, and part of it is the rhythm, but it's also about the touch, like how soft or firm you go. You just kind of have to listen to the music to feel what it wants." He experimented with the unit in front of him, alternating his approach to the drumhead from soft caresses to firm pats, all played to a steady beat. "Now you try. Start soft."

They worked together, Munie on her drum and Jackson on his, beginning with subtle, barely-there taps and graduating to medium-loud beats that sounded suspiciously like a pair of congas being played in skillful synchrony.

"Now you've got it! Try both hands!" Jackson threw down a complicated rhythm, and Munie stopped playing to laugh long and loud. He began laughing in response.

"That's, like, the best laugh I've ever heard," he managed between giggles.

"Thanks. And thanks for the lesson. Now I can say I've actually played something successfully! I really do need to get outside, though. My friend might be waiting."

As they stepped away from the stage and began making their way to the exit once again, Munie took in her companion's profile. She was intrigued by this unusual teenager, so sure of himself, so confident, yet completely unassuming. She had a feeling there was a lot more to this particular flower that was yet to unfurl.

"What's your plan, Jackson? Would you like to stay with music?"

He grinned. "Oh yeah. I'm planning to move to the States when I turn eighteen and get a record deal. But when I'm older, I'd love to be a music teacher."

"Really?"

"Absolutely."

"I think you'd be a wonderful teacher."

They'd reached the rear of the building and were standing on the dusk-drenched sidewalk in front of a loud, chaotic gaggle of squawking taxis. Munie turned and looked into the eyes of this remarkable young man whose talent and ambition were married to honest, endearing humility. A rare thing, indeed. "That's fantastic," she responded, both to him and to herself, a small smile of surprise on her face.

The sound of an ear-splitting horse whistle ended her reverie. Glenys was right next to her all of a sudden, one hand waving at a cab bearing a lighted "For Hire" sign and the fingers of the other hand poised at her mouth, preparing for another dose of sonic abuse. Munie turned to Jackson and extended her hand, which he took in a gentle handshake.

"I wish you all the luck in the world, Jackson. Much happiness to you. Take care."

"Thank you... ?" He looked at her quizzically.

"Oh! Munie. I'm Munie."

He strained visibly to hear her over the blare of car horns and the yells of people hailing them. "Thank you, Mindy," he said, smiling again in his charming way. Before she could correct him, he surprised her into silence by bending to kiss the top of her hand with chivalrous flair. Then he grinned into her eyes once more, turned, and walked back to his bandmates.

Glenys hadn't noticed; she was too busy yelling at the cabbie to move closer to the curb so that they could safely climb aboard. Once inside, the two women waved to the group of musicians as they drove away. For the rest of that evening, Munie wondered with gentle curiosity why Jackson Martinez Flores was still holding a space in her mind, and why her hand continued to thrum from the brief contact with his.

Songs on this Track

Quimbara: Words and music by Junior Cepeda; performed by Celia Cruz

The Way You Look Tonight: songwriter Jerome Kern; performed by Tony Bennett

2

—————

BLUE SKIES

October 2002
Via Clara, CA

"GLENYS, SHUT THE HELL UP."

"No, because I'm right."

"Fine, whatever. But that doesn't change the fact that I have to pay rent."

"Munie, you're miserable! Just look at this whole thing objectively. You want to write. You currently don't write a word. And you're doing math for a living."

"Accounting."

"A type of math."

"It's not that—it's her."

"Bullshit. Cruella is just the shite-flavored icing on a perfectly rotten cake. A manager who can't manage humanely is a boil on the arse of an organization. And mind you, it's their arse—not yours."

"Still."

"Still nothing! She trash-talked you behind your back to your client today. Your actual client!"

Munie just looked at her shoes, humiliation flooding through her at the memory. "I know."

"And what did that client say when he told you? He said that you deserved better, isn't that so?"

Her response came out as a sad sigh. "Yeah."

"There you have it! Just bloody quit, Mun. I've never seen you so blue, and I don't like it. It's only a job."

"It's the only job I have right now, Glen. No one else wants me." The tears that had been tangoing with her all day came out again for a little twist and dip, and she sniffled.

Glenys' voice came through the line a bit more softly. "Complete and utter bullshit, my love. You've had that journalism degree for five years now, and it's high time you used it. How many outlets have you spoken with in the last month?"

"None. I've been busy WORKING."

"With an organization that does not in any way deserve you. Sod them, take a week off, and start interviewing. You're brilliant, Munie, and there are many places for you to take your brilliance—without doing fucking math!"

Munie continued to make her way down Shaker Street with the phone at her ear and a lump in her throat, dodging the occasional skateboarder and smiling at a motley combination of dogs out for a late morning walk. The village of Via Clara soothed her—she enjoyed making the occasional one-hour escape from her tiny but expensive Glendale studio apartment to this renaissance blue collar town. The warehouses that were now artist's lofts, the bohemian coffee shops, and that feeling underneath it all of culture powered by a working-class hum were so different from Glendale's suburban sprawl or LA and its pretense. Via Clara just felt right.

"Listen, Doyle's out of town in a fortnight's time," Glenys continued, "so if you can feasibly finance a trip over, we can have a proper Ladies' Weekend, and I can also properly shake the bleeding—"

"Hey Glen, I gotta go. I want to hop into this place." She'd come to a stop in front of a perfectly retro vinyl shop, complete with LP covers in the windows. *Spin It Again Records* waved to her in worn neon lights. She was hungry for a distraction from horrible bosses, meaningless work, and yes, even well-meaning but overbearing friends—and this was one of those places she could get lost in for a while, she just knew it.

"All righty, then, ducks. Berate you again later. Love you—be good."

"Looking forward to it. Love you back." She shook her head with a smile, flipped closed her phone, wiped her eyes, and opened the door, the bell above it chiming her a welcome.

"Morning!" called a lean older gentleman from behind the desk. Decked out in a gray turtleneck with a few gold chains over it and a black leather cap, he looked like he'd stepped straight out of 1973. "Let me know if I can help ya."

Munie nodded her thanks with a smile, breathing in the singular smell of old vinyl and paper. It wrapped around her harried nerves like a warm blanket. Even the feeling of the smooth album covers against her fingers was reassuring, and the *floop-floop* sound they made as she flipped through them one at a time in the bin was like its own music.

There was some seriously vintage stuff here—Sinatra 1953?—as well as a lot of material she'd never even heard of. Just gazing at the images was like looking at a piece of art. Until the next one she picked up... *Bar Mitzvah Country Arrangements* by Manny "Tex" Goldstein.

Sometimes you can suppress a laugh or even pre-empt it, but other times it just bursts out in an exulted bleat. Munie had a belly laugh, and that's exactly what sang out across the mostly-empty store in that moment. *Mostly* empty, she emphasized to herself as she looked around immediately afterward—except for a middle-aged woman way across the room and a young man restocking albums literally two bin lengths away. Mortifying.

But all he did, to her immense relief, was to glance at the item in her hand and grin. And it was a beautiful grin.

"I TOLD Ray he should get rid of that thing. I think he actually keeps it for the laugh track, though." He had Sade in his hands, the sleeves of his flannel shirt rolled up to reveal a sphinx tattooed on the inside of his left forearm. A little knit cap barely covered his curly hair; Munie could see a few rebel curls peeking out here and there. His large brown eyes glimmered with mirth.

"Maybe I should buy it to play at dinner parties," she offered.

"Not if you want your guests to come back ever again."

She returned the smile he offered her. It felt good. There wasn't much in her world to smile about at the moment. She was sinking low into a soul-sucking job, and with no one at home to lighten the load, the balm of an old record store and a shared moment of lightness like this one were like drops of gold. She tried to keep the golden moment going for as long as possible.

"Do you work here? Maybe you could 'misplace' it someday."

"Oh, he'd know. It's just him and me, and ain't nobody going to shoplift that thing."

She belly-bleated again, though not quite as boisterously this time.

He laughed in response, twin dimples firing directly at her. "Damn, you have a great laugh." He extended a strong, warm hand to her; its energy rose in a gentle wave up her arm and somehow soothed her from head to toe. "I'm Jack. Jack Flores." There was something in his manner, his smile, and in the familiar way he introduced himself that struck a chord with her. But try as she might, she couldn't name that tune.

"Munie." She put the LP back in its spot and made a show of flipping through more albums, though her full interest was trained on him. "Have you worked here long?" He looked like he could even be in college.

"Only a couple of months," he replied. "I'm a musician, but that doesn't pay for much." He had moved to the next row and was now looking directly at her as he stocked. "You?"

She just sighed, reality pushing through the doors of the shop. "Long story. In a large nutshell, I crunch numbers for a living but I studied to be a journalist. I love music—not just listening to it, but studying it, talking about it, writing about it. I want to spend my career in that world. At least, that's my dream." Her eyes actually welled up as she spoke. Stupid tear ducts! She tried to hide it, but to no avail. He noticed and came over to her, placing a gentle hand on her shoulder.

"Hey," he offered with a soothing note in his voice, "wanna see the really good stuff? Ray won't stock it out here." When she balked, he backed up, hands raised in a gesture of innocence. "No ulterior motive, I promise. It's just behind that curtain."

A partly-closed drape at the back of the shop led to what looked like a break room. The chance to see some rare vinyl was definitely a draw, and a hard offer to pass up. Plus, since her tear ducts wouldn't seem to stifle it, a little dip away from the main room seemed like a good idea. Once there, Jack simply handed her a tissue and stood back, hands in his pockets and a gentle smile in his beautiful brown eyes.

"Thanks—and sorry," she murmured, trying to blow her nose as unobtrusively as possible.

"Nah—I get it. It hurts when there's something your heart wants to do, but your pocket won't agree to."

"Yeah, exactly. Couldn't have said it better. Same for you?"

"Yeah. Been in California for three years, and all I see down the line is gigging at night for pennies and spending every day here, staring at Country Bar Mitzvah covers."

She laughed again, kind of a half-laugh, half-cry where the brimming tears squeeze out any kind of way.

"Least I got you laughing again."

"True. And thanks for this. I never enjoy turning into a weepy puddle in the classic rock section."

"Then I'll make sure you're in the blues section next time." And they both laughed out loud. "I wasn't kidding, though," he continued, making his way to the far corner of the room, where a single large record bin stood against the wall. "This is where Ray keeps his really good stuff. You got to be in his personal contact list to get access, I think."

She walked over to where he stood and began to sift through the contents of the bin. "Billie Holiday?"

"Yeah! And check this out—Dean Martin signed by Sammy Davis, Jr."

"What?"

"You gotta hear the whole thing straight from Ray. He played upright bass on tour for those two in the early '70s, and he has some STORIES!"

Munie's mind reeled as she began to imagine simply sitting with Ray over a coffee and listening to what were bound to be amazing life experiences. "Oh man, I'd love to hear them sometime."

"And he loves to tell 'em too. Gives him life. I mean, I think he digs doing this," Jack continued, gesturing to the room around him, "but back then? That's when he was really on fire. He loved that life—that work—you can tell."

Aaaand just like that, the Sob Fairy was back. Munie turned her back to Jack in order to cry in front of a picture of Barry Manilow instead.

"Hey, hey, don't hide away like that." A gentle touch of his hand on her shoulder was all it took; the floodgates rolled open, and Munie was suddenly awash in tears. Having no idea what else to do, she simply turned toward him and buried her face against his shirt.

"You must think I'm mental," she whimpered, her words muffled against the flannel. He smelled clean and fresh and male ... so, so good. "And I hope Ray doesn't mind one of his customers having a full-on emotional breakdown in the back room."

She felt rather than heard his soft laugh as his arms came around her in a gentle embrace. His voice floated above her head, soothing and resonant. "Nah. Big Ed is out there with him. I heard him when he came in. Those two sit at the counter and bullshit like two crooked umpires at the playoffs."

She half-laughed again, a sound more closely resembling a soaked chortle. But his arms were strong and warm, his chest solid. There was just something about Jack Flores that made her feel at home. So she let him hold her.

She was just getting used to the muted thud of his heartbeat in the quiet room when he started to sing softly and slowly:

"Blue skies / Smiling at me / Nothing but blue skies / Do I see / Bluebirds / Singing a song / Nothing but bluebirds / All day long."

His voice was gorgeous, a low tenor with lightness and ease, the notes he created falling over her like snow. The sound found her somewhere she recognized, blanketing her in a frequency that was somehow familiar, and for that, all the more soothing:

"I never saw the sun shining so bright / Never saw things going oh-so right / Noticing the days hurrying by / When you're in love, my how they fly..."

He held her a teensy bit tighter, and she reciprocated as he rocked them gently back and forth, still singing, the sound filling her ears and the vibration caressing her cheek. Then finally:

"Blue days / All of them gone..." An effortless high note. *"Nothing but blue skies / From now on."*

They continued to hold each other in the ensuing silence, neither one wanting to let go first. At last, Munie raised her head.

Those eyes. Those beautiful, guileless eyes, looking at her completely and compassionately. Inches from her face.

Her gaze stole briefly to his lips, full and rich. He noticed, tightening his fingers around her waist ever so slightly, his eyes dropping to her mouth.

He bent toward her in slow motion. His forehead came to rest on hers, bringing them nose to nose so that they were breathing each other's breath. As exhausted as she was from the day's emotional roller coaster, her heart was still a kick drum against her ribs.

"Can I kiss you?" He whispered the words against her mouth, so close she could almost feel him shaping them.

Quiet. So quiet. But then, from the bowels of her broken spirit came the faint self-care act of "yes."

Yes.

He pulled away only to come back to her slowly, savoring every motion, lips parting just before they touched hers. So light, so good, so right. She moved her mouth against his, searching for more.

He gave her more, hands twining in her hair, his sweet mouth opening, tasting, taking more of what she offered him. His tongue found hers timidly at first, then more boldly as she reciprocated, savoring him right back. It was slow and deep and all-consuming.

But Jack was a gentleman, and began the denouement of their connection after only a little while, moving to gentler kisses, beautiful little sounds of affection, finishing with a kiss to to each corner of her mouth and each cheek. Then he was gazing at her again.

"You are so beautiful, Munie."

"Jack... I'm sorry... I shouldn't. I..."

The reality of where she was suddenly hit her like a mallet, and it dawned on her then and there that she was looking into the earnest eyes of a kid who was probably no older than his mid-twenties.

And she was thirty-one. Not good.

She turned around and began walking toward the curtain, but Jack grabbed her hand, not pulling but inviting her to pause, then guiding her body around to face him again.

"What's wrong? Did I hurt you?"

"Oh, Jack, no. You're so good. So sweet. No, you didn't hurt me at all. It's just that this..." she waved her arms around them like a cocoon, "it's just not... right."

"What? That was amazing right there. Some crazy kind of energy."

"I know, but Jack, I'm thirty-one years old."

"And?"

What are you, twenty..."

"I'm twenty-two."

"Oh shit." Munie rubbed her eyes in perhaps a subconscious effort to unsee his confused and slightly hurt expression, then slung her purse over her shoulder. "I really need to—"

He stepped toward her again, close. "Did you feel it?" His face still bore the same compassion, but now there was a new, urgent note of passion in his voice.

"Jack..."

"Did you feel it?" He took another step closer so that they were nose to nose again, his chest brushing against her breasts, brow furrowed with some indecipherable emotion. He waited for her answer.

"Yes," she whispered, though she wanted to yell it.

"Then that's it. That's all that matters. And Munie, I'm a grown man." With that, his mouth was on hers again, no longer slow and gentle, but urgent and seeking as he poured all that he wanted to tell her, to show her, into his kiss.

When she moaned against his mouth and wrapped her arms around his neck, he took that as his signal. His body was flush against hers as he lifted one of her arms and held it to the wall above her head. He pressed into her with everything he had, sucking at her neck, her collarbone, then back up to her mouth, hungry for every inch of her.

The next thing she knew, he was lifting her knee with his other hand, coming even closer, closer, tongue trailing down her sternum above the low v-line of her blouse. She found the firm roundness of his backside with her free hand and pushed, bringing his delicious want even closer to hers. And he did indeed want her, she realized.

Now her hand was under his shirt, skimming his smooth skin while he moaned into her mouth. She could totally have sex with him here, she realized, if she didn't... right this second... oh, his tongue in her ear... no, she absolutely had to...

"Stop."

Jack froze immediately, releasing her hand to raise both of his into the air. "Yeah," he nodded in a breathless exhale, "good call."

They left the back room one at a time even though there was no need—as Jack had predicted, Ray and Big Ed were still up front, alternately pointing at each other, pounding on the counter, and laughing.

He walked her to the door and then through it onto the sunny sidewalk.

"Will I see you again?" Good heavens, he was even more beautiful in the sunlight.

"I don't know, Jack."

"Munie..."

She remained quiet, even though every cell in her body was screaming "Yes please!"

At last, he pulled a pen from his pocket and wrote down his number. "Think about it, and if you decide it's OK for you, please call me, because Munie, I'd love to see you again." With that, he reached for her free hand, turned it toward him, and tenderly kissed the inside of her palm, making her knees go weak.

"That I can do. Goodbye, Jack." She turned away, feeling him watching as she walked down the street, a copy of John Coltrane's first album clutched in her hand, Jack's name and phone number scrawled into the upper right-hand corner.

SONGS on this Track

Blue Skies: Music and lyrics by Irving Berlin; performed by Ella Fitzgerald

3

SILENT LUCIDITY

June 2004
Los Angeles, CA

Munie demonstrated a third time, the earplug nestling snugly into her ear, but poor Glenys wasn't faring nearly as well.

"Squeeze, insert... fuck! Why does it keep falling out?"

"You have to really tuck it in there, so that it molds itself to the shape of your ear as it expands. If the foam doesn't expand right, it won't fill the hole, and it'll fall out again."

"Sounds like a chap I dated in college. Poor bloke. That was a short-lived fling." The plug fell out of her left ear again, landing with a mocking *plink* on the bar. "Blimey! Do I really need this nonsense anyway?" Glenys tossed the other plug onto the bar in a fit of frustration, then cursed again as it rolled into a spilled drip of beer.

Munie giggled and took a swig of her soda. "Yes. This is a rock club. Even if we're halfway toward the back—"

"Which we won't be, if I know you..."

"In any case, the amps will literally be feet away from us, and without protection you could damage your hearing permanently. That's what happened to Pete Townshend."

"Who? Hahahaha! Get it, Mun? Who?" Glenys smacked the bar in front of her with a hearty cackle, sending both earplugs onto the floor, which caused her to swear loudly once again. Munie merely reached into her bag for another set and passed it over.

"Cheers. And fine. Once I've finished my beer, I'll squeeze the shite out of these little buggers and make them fit as tightly as a swarthy Viking inside a Norse maiden." Munie guffawed as Glenys turned to address the gentleman next to her. "Oh yeah—sure. Have a seat. It's not taken."

A short, skinny young man with wild blond hair smiled his thanks and hopped onto the barstool, ordering a shot of bourbon and a Pabst Blue Ribbon. And Glenys, who had never met a stranger, launched right in without missing a beat.

"I'm just visiting LA, you know. My best mate here is moving to town from Glendale for a new job, and I'm helping her to get settled in. A bit sore in the arms from lifting boxes, mind you, but all in a good day's work. Do you come here often?"

Munie just shook her head and laughed.

Glenys' new friend, clad in a Ramones T-shirt and hopelessly ripped jeans, tattoos sprouting from seemingly everywhere, simply nodded, slammed down his shot, and took a swig of beer.

"I'm with the next band." He made a little drumroll motion with his hands. "Drums and background vocals."

"Brilliant!" Glenys stuck out a hand. "Pleasure. I'm Glenys, and this is Munie. *Un nuevo Angelino*, as they say." There was absolutely nothing Latin in Glenys' pronunciation. "Mun here is a music journalist, you know."

Apparently unfazed by her butchery of the Spanish language, the gentleman rubbed a hand against his jeans as if to clean it, then extended it to her. "Right on. I'm Thumper."

Although Glenys had a poker face for the ages, there was absolutely no way Munie could keep from laughing, so she bent forward, away from the bar, pretending to rummage through her purse as she silently shook with glee.

"So then, "*Thoomperrrh*" (it was even more hilarious in Glenys' Scottish brogue, and Munie was now literally crying into her hand-bag), "have you played with this band for long?"

He seemed genuinely happy that she was interested, and smiled wide. "Oh yeah, for a couple of years now. We just do cover songs, though."

"I love cover bands! What are we going to hear tonight, then?"

"Oh! Well, we're changing it up a little from the usual set list, since we have a sub on guitar." He leaned in and stage-whispered to the women. "Our regular guy has the crabs real bad." Munie actually whimpered—she had no more giggles left to use.

"Oh dear." How Glenys was not on the floor by now she had no idea.

"Yeah. It's OK, though. This dude—I think his name is Martin or Martinez or something—can totally shred. I guess he's more of a jazz cat, but whatever. He can still rock!" Thumper flashed the universal rock -n-roll symbol with his right hand for emphasis. "He's got one hell of a voice too. I mean, like, you've got your righteous wailers like Michael Sweet, Miljenko from Steelheart ..."

"Sebastian Bach?" Munie creaked from the depths of her purse.

"Whoa, yeah! Right on. That dude's so good he almost makes me want to switch teams, know what I mean?"

Munie leaned away and whimpered again, wondering why she ever tried to come up for air in the first place.

"But yeah. This Martin guy's totally up there vocally. We usually cover Zeppelin, Van Halen, the Stones, stuff like that. But tonight we're gonna add on a couple of things for him special—Queensrÿche, maybe even Heart or some Journey. Chicks love Journey."

Munie's chest was now physically hurting from the effort to contain the belly laugh that was begging to be let out.

"Oooh—some solid choices there!" Glenys just kept rolling along, smooth as silk.

"Right on. It's all great, but guess what?"

"What?" Glenys' eyes were wide with genuine fascination and her smile huge, as if she were chatting with an excited toddler.

"I'm writing my own stuff now too."

"Really?"

"Yeah!" He looked so proud. "It's kinda like Chicago meets Pestilence."

Even Glenys wobbled a little on her stool with that one. For Munie, recovery of her decorum was officially no longer possible. Tears careening down her face, she croaked a strained "Excuse me" over her shoulder and removed herself to laugh her ass of in the ladies' room. Or in front of it, at least. One cardinal rule of hanging out at dive bar rock clubs was that you do NOT, under any circumstances, use the facilities.

She ended up ducking outside instead to catch some fresh air, even though the lights were already flickering to indicate the impending start of the show. By the time she returned—calm, clear-eyed and devoid of makeup smears—things were already underway and the crowd was going nuts for the song she'd just missed.

Glenys was about two-thirds of the way toward the back of the venue, to the far right. Oh well. At least the sound would be good at this distance. Munie pressed her way into the throng of humans and took her place beside Glenys, who, earplugs now correctly inserted, was horse-whistling, whooping, and shaking her head in wonderment.

"Fucking hell, Mun! I think you may have just missed the best part of the show!" she screamed. "Martin the Sub just kicked the ever-loving shite out of the vocal on 'Silent Lucidity.'"

Glenys pointed to the far side of the stage; Munie could vaguely see the side profile of a well-shaped, almond-skinned young man in jeans and a pink tee-shirt, its short sleeves rolled up above his biceps Arthur Fonzarelli style. He was switching out an acoustic guitar for a cherry red Stratocaster, a cigarette tucked behind his ear. Shit. When Glenys got that excited, it had to be good, and she didn't even like

Queensrÿche. Munie realized she'd just missed a moment. She was slightly angry with herself, but mollified by the fact that it was just the beginning of the show—there might be more such moments still to come.

Sadly, Martin the Sub, or whoever he was, had no more solo vocals in the set—just a lot of excellent guitar playing. She loved that he didn't show off much, other than a little sprinkle of dancing, gesturing, and some well-placed interplay with the ladies in the audience. As the show went on, Munie noted that a good portion of his flirtation was aimed at a blond in the front row. He repeatedly headed right over to her, playing to her, making eye contact, even kneeling in front of her at one point. But outside of those little moments, he didn't really go in for the typical rock music shenanigans, but rather maintained his place at the far end of the stage, working out while a cigarette burned in the head stock of his guitar.

After the show, Munie watched another cigarette burn—this time from between Glenys' fingers as they stood outside the venue. She'd started smoking in college, and although Munie hated it and had tried at every opportunity to get her to quit, so far it had been a no-go. But she wasn't about to leave her friend alone in the alley outside a crowded LA club late at night either, so she found herself leaning against the wall and trying not to breathe too deeply.

Looking around, she spotted a familiar form outside the other exit door, about thirty feet down the alley. Pink shirt, sleeves still rolled up, leaning against the wall with his own cigarette between his lips.

"Oh, there's Martin the Sub."

"Hey?"

"The guitarist."

Glenys cast her eyes in the direction Munie indicated just as Martin turned his back to them. "Ah yeah. My, that's a nice, tight arse he's got there."

"Glen, seriously, he's a baby."

"Well, he's a baby with some smooth moves, then, I'll give him that." Martin the Sub was now back in profile, talking with an attractive young Asian woman standing close enough to him to indicate that they knew each other fairly well. Munie watched him smile at the woman, caress her cheek, then move in and kiss her slowly on the mouth.

"All right, so maybe the blond in the front row isn't his girlfriend," Munie posited. The woman smiled up at him, said something else, kissed him gently, and walked away. He simply leaned back against the brick wall and continued smoking.

Munie couldn't see his face clearly from the side, especially from that distance, but something struck her as familiar in the way he moved and generally how he carried himself. Each time he took a drag on his cigarette, she could just see a dimple appear on his cheek. That dimple was familiar too. Where had she seen him before?

They were just about to leave their post and head home when a second woman walked up to him. She was tall—model tall—with long brown hair flowing over her shoulders and a black mini dress barely concealing a brick house body.

His smile this time was a surprised one—kind of sweet, Munie had to admit. Maybe this was his sister? A friend? Nope. You don't open-mouth kiss your friend and grab her ass unless it's THAT kind of friendship. What the hell was this, an episode of *The Bachelor*? Now he had both hands on her face and was coming in for a thorough examination of her tonsils.

"Fuck's sake! What's he going to do next—host an orgy at the McDonald's across the street?" Glenys took a final puff, tossed her cigarette butt onto the pavement, stamped it out, and heaved a sigh. "This is just depressing. He's getting more action in ten minutes than I've had in a year." She snorted and poked Munie in the ribs. "Make you want to rethink having broken off the engagement with Michael?"

"Hell no. No action is better than the wrong action, Glen." She watched as Martin the Sub and his friend continued making out, arms now twined around each other, her hands in his hair, and both of his hands on her ass. Just as Munie was beginning to wonder how long the show might go on, the couple pulled apart, turned onto the sidewalk and headed into the sunset together, the woman taking hits from his cigarette as they strolled along into the night. Ah, LA.

Songs on this Track

Silent Lucidity: Songwriter Chris DeGarmo; performed by Queensrÿche

4

A CASE OF YOU

June 2008
Los Angeles and Laurel Canyon, CA

IT TOOK ALMOST FOUR YEARS AS A MUSIC JOURNALIST WITH *LIFT Magazine* for Munie to finally be authorized to fraternize with the rich and famous. However, rich and famous in her case equated to newly-discovered talent and onetime celebrities now contemplating a second or third comeback. The details didn't matter, though—she was finally settled into a career doing what she loved, and it was just getting better by the day.

Tonight's assignment was an easy one. She was covering a small, informal reception for new artists under the *Theta* label—a simple drinks mixer in one of the social rooms within *Theta's* expansive *L.A.* office complex. The party was comprised of four or five newly-signed folks, their *Theta* 'Work Buddies,' and a handful of lesser-known-and-therefore-less-annoying music journalists, to include one Rai Paley. The task list from her editor, Latisha, was a walk in the park: 1. take in the details of the event; 2. grab a few quotes from the *Theta* reps and artists; 3. write an article; and 4. have fun. Not a bad day at the office, indeed.

She was exchanging pleasantries with one of the Work Buddies when she saw him leaning against a column with a bourbon rocks in his hand, laughing and carrying on with another artist. He was dressed in that casual but chic style that only truly sexy men can pull off—black jeans, polished shoes, and a fitted silk shirt with enough buttons undone to reveal a smooth, broad chest bearing a few simple gold necklaces. His rolled-up sleeves revealed three tattoos on his forearms, though she couldn't make out any of them. He had a close-ish cropped haircut that just barely tamed a tight, all-over-every-where Afro, and silky smooth skin that was likely not the result of expensive creams, but simply the product of being young.

Sometimes people have a feeling that they've met someone before, and that was this moment for her. She was mesmerized by him somehow—the way he waved his hands in the air when he talked, how he swiped his fingers around his mouth after he smiled, even the way he sipped his drink. He was easy in his skin, easy with his laughter—he just flowed. And she was utterly lost in it.

Then he turned his head, as if he sensed her watching, and his eyes locked on hers. Warm and brown, guileless and direct, they stared straight into her, a small lift at his lips. As soon as she saw those eyes, she knew him immediately. He was dressed in the guise of a celebrity instead of a record store stock boy, but it was him. She was one thousand percent sure. Jack. Excusing himself from his companion, he roused from his leaning place and sauntered over to her, holding her gaze all the while.

"Hey."

"Hi." Munie smiled at him with what could have been either familiar repartee or polite introduction, waiting for some sign of recognition from him, some glimmer of remembrance. But there was none.

He inclined his head toward her, the light in his eyes dancing seductively. "I'm Gene."

A stage name, she immediately thought to herself. There had been a Gene on the bio sheet from Latisha. Gene... Gene...

"Coltrane, right?" He smiled a wide grin, dimples lighting up both sides of his face at once. He was so handsome it rocked her a little. "That's it. And you're..."

She made her decision, pulling out her own professional moniker instead of the name she had once shared with him. "I'm Rai. Rai Paley."

"It's a pleasure to meet you, Rai. A real pleasure." He extended his hand, she took it, and a circuit of that same something she'd felt in Via Clara... what the hell was it?... jolted through her. He felt it too, she realized; he straightened up a little but kept his hand around hers. Meanwhile, his eyes shamelessly skied over her body, savoring her from tip to toes. She found she didn't care. Actually, she realized with a tiny wave of embarrassment, she enjoyed watching him take her in like that.

There were a few moments of get-to-know you banter—congratulations from her on his signing with *Theta*, questions from him about the kind of journalism she was involved with—but when he asked if he could refresh her drink, and their fingers grazed again as he took her empty glass, the conversation shifted to a silent, tacitly understood chorus of "I Want You."

She wanted him indeed, in a visceral, almost animal way she'd never felt before—a sensation even more powerful than it had been in the back room of that record store. His indescribable scent made her heady, and her eyes couldn't decide whether to focus on that unapologetic stare, his full, delicious lips, or the well-made and strong hands she wanted roaming all over her again. In the end, it was the hands, which held his phone number on a scrap of paper. When his car came to take him away, he leaned in and kissed her cheek, whispering "please call me" close into her ear. They stayed in that position for a beat or two longer than necessary, soaking in the heat and the connection between them.

Munie Paley had a moral moment with herself when she got home that night. First of all, she was a relationship girl, not a meet-you-on-Saturday-and-see you-naked-on-Sunday sort of individual (at least from his perspective). Second, the fact that he didn't remember her cast a shadow on this whole interchange. Should she really be jumping into bed with someone who didn't even recall having had a truly intimate moment with her?

Based on the electricity of their last exchange, she had a feeling that if she called him, that's exactly what would happen, moral barometer be damned. Even the thought of seeing what was under that silk shirt was making her a little light-headed as she lolled on the couch in her Bart Simpson PJs. Ridiculous. There was only one way to sort this out.

"What." Reasonably speaking, it was 6 am in Edinburgh, so Glenys was allowed to be a little grumpy.

"I want to have sex."

"Can't help you there, ducks," Glenys yawned into the other end of the phone. Munie could hear things popping and cracking over the line as Glenys was most likely cat-stretching in bed. "I'm not equipped for what you're looking for, even were I there with you in the swamp."

"LA isn't a swamp," Munie retorted as she peered into the fridge for the eighth time, looking for anything labeled "Food to Curb my Lust."

"It is. A swamp of banality and greed."

"That's beautiful."

"But back to this sex—anyone in particular you have in mind?"

Glenys knew about the fiery interchange in Via Clara six years before, but instead of mentioning that Jack was back, Munie decided in the moment, for a reason she couldn't pinpoint, to leave that fact out of the conversation. The abridged version came out in one sentence around a mouthful of granola bar. "A musician. I met him last night it was insane and hewantsmetocallhimwhatshouldIdo?!"

"Oh the label thing, yeah? Civilian or rock star?"

"Neither," Munie crunched. "Kind of embryonic celebrity, maybe?"

"Is he quite hot?"

"You have no idea. Glen—when he touched my hand there were literal sparks."

"And that's bad?"

"If I call him I might, like, jump on him, and I don't do that! Plus, he's a sort-of celebrity, and I'm supposed to be just writing about them, not riding them!"

"Have you been assigned to write about him?"

"No."

"Are you authoring his biography or some such?"

"No."

"Then I don't see the problem. Plus, my darling, unless I'm out of date regarding your personal life, it has been quite a while."

"Thanks for the reminder." She grunted in frustration. "I don't know what to *dooooo*."

"Munie love, it is entirely too early to beat around the bush, so I'll be blunt. You need a good shag, and this bloke sounds as though he'd be able to deliver handily. Do *him*. Just be safe. Goodbye."

Click.

Good old Glenys. A woman without a filter. Occasionally a pain in the ass, but at the end of the day, a huge asset in a best friend.

Munie unwrapped another granola bar, groaned, and texted the number on the scrap of paper.

> Hi—it's Rai.

His response came in a little after 1 am.

> Hey Rai—sorry just finished the set. You good?

> Yeah—thanks.

She literally could not think of anything else to say. But just as she began metaphorically stomping her feet in frustration, his next text popped in.

> Can I call you?

> Sure.

She deliberately waited until the second ring to pick up—no reason to seem overly eager, even though that was exactly how she felt. "Hello?"

"Hey." Shit, even his phone voice was sexy.

"Good show?"

"I guess so. Sometimes I wish I could split myself in half and see it from the audience's perspective, you know?"

She laughed a little. "I can understand that. Maybe I have it easier, since I can read my own stuff as many times as I want. But come to think of it, that could be my problem!"

He chuckled, and she smiled at the sound, snuggling up under a blanket to hear more.

They talked for the next two hours. He made her laugh until tears rolled down her cheeks with stories about the stupid joke contest he and his band members were having. He was giggling so hard at times that he had trouble getting out some of the words, and she could just imagine how his face looked all joy-contorted.

He asked all about her job, and even had a few anecdotes about some of the artists she'd written about. He had a deep respect for every one of them, and never had a single negative thing to say. She marveled that he had such a rich well of experience to share for someone his age in the industry. And there was something deep about him in general, a hidden compartment under the surface that she couldn't see. But Munie could read people, and she knew it was there, that there were layers in him just waiting to be peeled back.

———————-

THE NEXT DAY was supposed to be lunch at a little bistro near his house—at least that's what they'd agreed on their late-night phone call—but lunch didn't last long. No food was eaten.

She walked up to *Frank's* to find Jack standing alone at their agreed landmark, under a grape arbor down the path from the restaurant entrance, hands in his jeans pockets, a cream-colored cashmere hoodie on to beat the unseasonably cool LA morning. He looked delicious. Should she shake his hand, she wondered? Kiss him on the cheek? What the hell does one do in this kind of situation?

As she approached him, he walked toward her, a smile in his eyes and on his face. But before she could determine her best move, he was coming in for a quick hello peck on the lips.

Bad idea. That little taste turned into a tornado. He drew back only to come to her again in slow motion, hands to her cheeks, turning her head for deeper access. Full, soft lips caressing and probing, covering her in their warm, erotic movement. Her arms went around him, pulling him toward her. Soon it was teeth nipping, tongues exploring, bodies pressed together, right there for the world to see.

All she could taste was him—mint and a faint tinge of strawberry. Familiar but new all at once. All she could smell was that clean, male fragrance. Just like before, his solid, smooth form felt incredible against her. All she wanted was his mouth on hers, over and over and over and over...

"Should we go in?" His voice was ragged and he was as breathless as she was, his forehead resting against hers.

If there had ever been a debate in her mind before, it was well and truly over now. "No," she whispered.

They practically fell through the front door of his house, their bodies pressed against the foyer wall—first hers, then his, then hers again, all giggles and panting and fumbling fingers. Then a mad and messy dash to the bed. She was intoxicated by him— the smooth, perfect skin under her hands, those pillowy lips skimming her shoulder, the dimples peeking out from between her legs. He whispered words of wonder in her ear, smiled across her skin as his hands explored her curves, and looked deep in her eyes as he pushed deep inside, finally feeding the fire between them.

The gold chain on his chest chimed a rhythm against her skin as he moved over her, his mouth humming into hers, her fingers hopelessly tangled in his curly hair. She'd never been to bed with a man before so soon after meeting him, but this was something chemical, something electric. She'd never made love half-dressed before either, but there they were, his gray tee shirt sliding against her bra to the syncopated rhythm of his hips.

Oh my stars, those hips, she thought to herself before she completely lost her mind to the groove.

Afterward, as they lay on their backs catching their breaths, she took in the view around her. The room was huge and light-filled, with high ceilings and pricy coverings, a two thousand-dollar overstuffed chair in the corner with his now-discarded tee shirt thrown over it. Floor to ceiling windows with no treatments. An empty bookshelf. A walk-in closet that probably had only a few clothes in it.

"Lunch?" he ventured. They both laughed out loud.

"Oh my gosh I can't believe we just did that."

"I can. I've been thinking about you nonstop since last night. Seriously." He turned to face her, head resting on his hand, a smile on his face. "What have you done to me, woman?" he quipped with a raised eyebrow. Just then, his stomach gave an audible growl, and they both erupted in laughter.

"Other than make you hungry?" she returned.

"Right. Let's take care of that. Be right back." He rose, naked as his birthday, and sauntered out of the room, returning a minute later with a container of grapes, a jug of water, and two glasses. "It ain't *Frank's*, but—"

"—it's perfect," she finished, sitting up in the bed with the sheet draped around her torso.

After a few silently luxurious moments of noshing, he rubbed his hand down his mouth thoughtfully. "OK," he offered, "you said you can't believe we just made love like that. Why?"

Agggghhhh, she ogled to herself, *he even uses the term 'making love.'* "I guess … I guess just because it was so fast. I mean, aside from one five-minute in-person conversation and one long phone call, we don't really even know each other… I mean… other than physically… oh geez…"

He just grinned and slowly pushed a large red grape into his mouth—likely the same color as her face at the moment. "Keep going," he encouraged playfully.

"I mean, that's really it. We're basically strangers." *According to you,* she added silently with a small pang. She explored his gaze once again for some hint of recognition, some memory of their interchange in Via Clara, but there was nothing there.

"Strangers, huh? Well then, let's fix that. Tell me five things about you."

"Like what?"

He waved another grape in the air. "An easy one. Where were you born?"

"Santa Monica."

"No shit."

"Yep—California girl through and through."

"Wow. Blonde and everything." He reached out, took a lock of her long golden hair gently between his fingers, and let it glide through, a rapt expression on his face.

"I'm not a natural blonde."

His gaze roved overtly down to her lap and back up to her eyes. "I know," he grinned. His voice was low and sultry, and her face felt like it was about five hundred degrees.

If he noticed her embarrassment, he delicately ignored it and moved on. "Number two. Favorite meal."

"Oooh that's hard. I love food." She mused for a moment. "It's got to be crab legs with drawn butter and a cold local beer, at an outdoor table right on the docks in Fisherman's Wharf."

"Nice! Number three. Name a song that makes you feel all nostalgic."

"Easy. It's either that one love song by Richard Marx, or—what??"

Jack was clutching his heart and pulling a face of severe mock emotional pain. "Please, baby, put me out of my misery. What's the other option?"

"Oh, for pity's sake. Musicians." She rolled her eyes dramatically and shook her head. "'Love Shack.' B-52s."

He sat back upright, magically cured of his fake coronary affliction. "OK, now that I can get on board with. Next question. Favorite person to interview so far."

Without hesitation, she replied, "Nickles Boone. Amazing guy. So kind, so funny, and every one of his stories is completely epic."

He straightened up, almost disrupting the sheet covering his lap, obviously impressed. "Aw man, Nickles is the truth! I only met him once—we jammed with a bunch of other folks at a charity event. Damn I'd love to work with him again. The man's a genius. OK, last question ..."

"I'm ready."

"What do you want to be when you grow up?"

She laughed, then realized he was serious. "In what way?"

"In all the ways. In your career, in your life, where do you see yourself. How do you want to... be?"

The depth of his question surprised her, but his face gave no expression other than earnest interest, as free of embellishments as his partially-covered naked body. She saw that he expected her to answer fully, and he very much wanted to hear all she had to say.

"Wow," she exhaled. "No one's ever actually asked me that before." She picked up a grape, considering.

"Well," she started, trying to find the words she wanted, "people fascinate me. I like to try and understand them, but at the same time, I'm not great with too much exposure to them, if that makes any sense. It's just a lot."

"I get it. Say more." He had abandoned the grapes and was now fully focused on her, elbow propped on his bent knee, head resting in his hand.

"A partner, maybe, that would be nice someday, but not absolutely necessary."

"Kids?"

"No. I just never had that desire."

"So you like what you do, you like where you are, and want to live on your own terms. Yeah?"

"Yeah. Pretty much. You're good at this, Coltrane." She smiled, taking in his smooth, broad chest and the finely-drawn music staff tattoo decorating his left pectoral. She let her gaze rove over strong shoulders and well-defined arms, then reached out to lightly trace the contours of a colorful parrot tattoo decorating his right bicep. His skin was so warm, so smooth. "You could be a journalist."

He just smiled, his eyes moving from her face to the hand on his arm, his expression changing from earnest to hungry as he took in her sheet-clad form.

"Come to think of it," she continued, moving to sit astride him and placing a slow kiss on his lips, "you're good at a lot of things." She felt him move under her as they continued to kiss, hands seeking one another again.

"Can I ask a bonus question?" His voice at her ear came out lower this time, huskier.

"Go for it."

"Can I see that natural color up close again?"

The container of grapes hit the floor with a plunk as Jack yanked the sheet away from both of them, rolled their bodies toward the mattress, and pulled Munie's pelvis toward his mouth with one arm, his lust-black gaze fixed on the morsels before him.

"Five questions," she breathed shortly thereafter, having just come down from a powerful climax, Jack's head still resting on her thigh as he tasted in and around her center. Although she loved it, he'd been languorously nibbling for a while, and things were getting sensitive.

"Mmmmm?"

"My turn to ask you."

He laughed, his hot breath on her tenderest spot. "If you insist." He pulled himself back up to the pillows slowly, kissing a trail from the inside of her thigh all the way to her sternum, and rested on his side.

She turned toward him so that they were face to face. "Favorite color."

"Blue."

"Ocean or mountains?"

"Ocean. I'm from the Bahamas."

She casually twirled one of his curls around her finger as she spoke. "First song you ever learned in order to woo a girl."

"Oooh! Good question!" He thought for a moment, then suddenly hopped up off the bed, grabbing an acoustic guitar from the corner of the room. Then, sitting bare-ass naked at the foot of the bed, he began to strum and sing. To her utter surprise, the song he eased into with the softness of a cloud was Joni Mitchell's 'A Case of You.' He began at almost a whisper, his fingers gently caressing the strings and his voice weaving back and forth into a falsetto that brought tears to her eyes.

Even as she listened, Munie realized this was a moment she'd remember forever—the sight of him, firm and smooth and beautiful all at once, the sound of his perfectly light and soulful tone filling the room. Tenderness with just a pinch of gravel. Sincere and just as stripped-down as they were. As he sang, he looked at her. Sang TO her. She never wanted it to stop.

He played through the entire song, and when he finished, there was a long silence. Finally, Munie found her voice.

"I'll bet it worked, didn't it?" she offered quietly, finding it difficult to speak around the frog in her throat. He laughed, dropped the guitar and pulled her close, sending them both back into the pillows.

"You have two more questions," he offered, stroking her back softly.

"Ah yes," she replied, placing little kisses down his neck. "If you weren't a musician, what would you do?"

"Teach," he said without hesitation.

"Really?" She drew back to look at him.

"You're surprised?"

"A little. Why?"

"Lots of kids where I grew up have no opportunity for a good education. I got lucky with music—I had an 'out.' I'd love to make sure no other kid needs an escape route in order to make it."

She kissed him full on the lips, falling for him a little bit more every second. This could be dangerous. Time to lighten the moment, she decided.

"How old were you when you moved here?"

"Nineteen."

"Where's your accent?" she teased, playfully grazing a hand over his firm backside as she spoke and punctuating her question with a playful squeeze.

He grinned, pressing her closer. "Calm ya passion, gyal. Ya fixin' me real good now, ya know."

Wrong thing to ask. She could feel her heart rate pick up, thrumming against his chest, and she could feel him respond against her body lower down.

"Last question," he whispered into her mouth.

She looked behind him at the empty bookshelf, all thought leaving her head as he began to stroke her nipple with guitar-callused fingers.

"Your shelf is empty."

"Mmmmm?" His hand lower, spanning her belly, gently rolling her onto her back.

"Your shelf." She closed her eyes as her breath hitched, a give-away to the attentions of his hand, now between her legs. "You don't have any books."

"Mmmmm." He simply smiled, bent his head to taste her breast, and moved his body over hers, positioning himself in just the right spot.

"What are you going to fill it with?"

One smooth thrust and she was back in the stars.

Two hours and one nap in the sun later, they both awoke to the sound of her phone buzzing with a text message. There was an article she needed to write about yesterday's reception, and of course she hadn't started it yet. And of course it was due tonight. He headed to the bathroom and she got dressed. He pulled on some boxers and the tee shirt from earlier, and asked her if she wanted something more to eat before heading out. She declined and they embraced one more time at the front door.

"When do you leave?" she asked as she breathed him in again.

"Tuesday," he replied, cupping her ass one last time. "But I'm back in two months. I'll call you. I want to see you again. I want to see you a lot." One more deep and mind-bending kiss. One more sip of the alchemy between them.

"I want that too," she sighed into his mouth.

He never called.

SONGS **on this Track**

Love Shack: Lyrics and music by the B-52s; performed by the B-52s

A Case of You: Songwriter Joni Mitchell; performed by Joni Mitchell

5

LET'S GET IT ON

November 2012
Hell's Kitchen, New York, NY

THERE IS VERY LITTLE THAT IS MORE BEAUTIFUL THAN A PERFECT BLACK olive and mushroom slice in New York City when you're completely ravenous, especially when washed down with a cold bottle of root beer. In fact, Munie decided she was so in love with this particular slice that she just had to share it. Sadly, her image-only text message was not received with matching euphoria from its recipient.

How dare you?

Looks good, eh?

Your effrontery is positively galling, especially as you are well aware that pizza anywhere in the UK tastes like donkey bollocks.

Munie had to focus hard in order not to spit her root beer across the tiny restaurant.

Then I shouldn't tell you that I'm eating this particular slice in a hidden pizza joint in Hell's Kitchen about as big as your living room, right?

Munie Paley, we are no longer friends.

This last message from Glenys was followed by a middle finger emoji, kiss emoji, and heart emoji. Munie chuckled as she put down her phone, lifted her slice, and, with a look of pure rapture, took an enormous bite.

"Oh, you are so beautiful," she cooed to her food, her mouth full almost to capacity.

"Thanks."

The voice came from the seat right next to her, startling her so that she almost toppled off her own stool, pizza dropping from her hands back onto the grease-stained paper plate in front of her.

"Whoa. Sorry. Didn't mean to scare you like that." He was laughing, but in a sincere, apologetic way. "You OK?"

"Geez," she breathed, gathering her wits about her. "I had no clue you were there." Munie was mortified that she'd been so caught up in her food as to not notice someone sitting right next to her, much less such an attractive man. She shook her head with a laugh, turned to get a better look at what she'd been missing, and did an immediate double-take. It was him. Again. Jack. But as she dug into those familiar and just-as-beautiful-as-ever brown eyes, she found not a sliver of recognition coming back to her. How was that even possible?

She stared at him silently for a moment, anger brewing deep in her gut. Maybe it was a ruse? Once again, she decided she'd play along. "I recognize you."

"Gene Coltrane." The way he said it was informal, as if he knew she knew him. Maybe he did remember her after all. She was just about to bring up their previous smoldering connection when he dumped a proverbial bucket of water on the fire. "I'm a musician. You may have seen my face somewhere."

"Ah. Right." *Unbelievable,* she marveled to herself, slightly disgusted at his cluelessness. Yet something egged her on. "What are you doing out and about like this, all alone? Aren't you afraid of getting mobbed?"

"That's why I'm back here in the corner. I recognized you from the Met benefit thing last night, figured you'd be cool."

"You recognized me?" Her heart began to beat just a little more rapidly; she could feel the pulse at her throat.

"Yeah. You don't see that color red too often—especially in a short haircut. It was too cute to forget." He winked at her, a smile pulling at one side of his mouth, and she withered a little inside. "Plus, I heard nobody's here this early."

Seemingly unaware of the dejection he was causing, Jack picked up his pepperoni slice, took a bite even bigger than Munie's, and moaned out loud. It sounded too good. She began to imagine what he might have looked like in his tux less than twenty four hours ago, but then, annoyed at her body's blatant disloyalty to her heart, she quickly pulled her head out of her haunches. He turned her on much too easily. But even so, she had absolutely no space for love-'em, leave-'em, and forget 'em Casanovas in her life.

"How'd you hear about this place, anyway?" she asked, taking a cooling swig of her Boylan's.

"From Nickles Boone. He grew up in this neighborhood. You?"

She laughed out loud. "Same."

"No way!"

"He told me to be here at four sharp, as soon as they open, when it's nice and empty."

"Oh yeah? He told me to be here at four too, but," he sat up straighter and huffed out his chest in mimic fashion, "'cause only assholes like you go there that early, baby.'"

Munie laughed loudly again at his spot-on Nickles impression, and watched him toss another relaxed dazzler back at her, his shoulders shaking in merriment, twin dimples flashing like headlights. He was beautiful, no way around it. And she did really like talking with him. No harm in making conversation, she supposed.

"But Nick's wrong," he continued, adjusting his smile to something with a touch of hot pepper; she could feel it on her tongue. "This place clearly isn't just for assholes like me. At least not at four pm." He met her gaze and she didn't even think about looking away, even though she was already beginning to get tipsy on his eyes.

"I'm glad to hear that."

He came just a little closer, and the circuit of energy around him met her own with a palpable frisson. "What's your name, Red?"

You should already know what it is.

As she looked at his open, interested face, a porch where the lights were on but clearly no one with a memory was at home, Munie decided that he didn't get the honor of her name this time—either her work name or her personal one. Instead, she gave him the word that first popped into her mind. "I'm Glenys."

"Cheers, Glenys," he replied with a tip of his head, bringing the neck of his bottle to meet hers in the air.

—-

"ROUND TWO. ON ME." Jack plopped down a second slice of pizza in front of each of them, along with another root beer for her and a Sam Adams for him.

"Well thank you kindly, Mr. Coltrane."

"Anytime. So where were we?"

"It's your question. But wait a minute. Before we start, why are you still wearing that thing?" She indicated the heavy leather jacket still wrapped around him.

"Because I'm fucking freezing!"

She laughed openly at him. "Come on, man. It's almost sixty degrees outside, the fire from the pizza oven is throwing out heat like a torch, and this place is all of about 700 square feet."

"Girl, I'm from the Caribbean and I live in LA. I don't do cold." He looked down at his chest. "But you're right—surer than shit I'm getting sauce on this thing." As he struggled out of the jacket to reveal a form-fitting, baby blue Henley, a waft of his delicious scent caught Munie's nose, and she was suddenly too warm, even with her hoodie already on the seat beside her. When he followed up that show by removing his cap to free an adorable riot of tight, dark curls, the weight and texture of which she remembered feeling between her fingers and against the insides of her thighs, she wanted to smack him for turning her on again.

"Better?" she squeaked. *Good grief, woman,* she scolded herself, *get a grip. There is no way you're going there again.*

"Yeah, good idea. All right—want to go back to food, stick with music, or go somewhere else?"

She took a bite, considering. "Music's good. We've covered food pretty well. Plus, to be fair, I'm getting too full to be objective."

"I hear that. OK, cool. My question is ... first album you ever owned."

She only had to think for a split second. "*Donna Summer's Greatest Hits.*"

"Oh! Very solid."

"You?"

"*Thriller.*"

"Perfect."

"Yeah. OK, you're up. Hit me, girl."

She rubbed her hands together, thinking. "Favorite cover song. Popular music lane only."

"Oof—tough one." He was pensive for a few seconds, then sat up straight. "Luther. 'Superstar.' You can't beat it." He raised his gaze to some point in the air in front of him, squinted his eyes to half mast, and began to sing that iconic first line. All feeling, all soul. "I mean, it's doesn't get better than that." Given the mild swoon that befell her as a result of his smooth crooning, Munie had to agree. "How 'bout you?"

Munie saw one more opportunity to jog his memory, and grabbed it. "Do you know Joni Mitchell's 'A Case of You'? The Prince cover is gorgeous."

He lit up, a warm smile spreading across his face, and her hopeful heart skipped a beat.

"Oh yeah," he replied in a sultry exhale, his expression dreamy. "Back in high school, I had a crush on this girl who was a big Joni Mitchell fan. I mean, a huge crush. Massive. I learned that song just so that I could sing it to her on our first date."

Dejection almost blocking her windpipe, Munie managed just one word. "And?"

"And she said no to the date. Great song though. I've played it a couple of times since—once on tour ... tryna remember the other time. Why the hell can't I call it up?" He stared at his beer bottle for a second, as if he thought it would conjure up the memory; at the same time, Munie realized that there had to be something keeping him from remembering her. The realization gave her solace, if only in small measure. "Ah shit. Sorry. Maybe it'll come to me later." He took a a swig and shook his head energetically, curls bouncing every-where. "My turn."

Munie heaved a sigh, still despondent but now with a small side of acceptance that put a fresh layer of levity into her perspective. Perhaps there was a "why" after all, even if she wouldn't ever know its composition. Her demeanor slightly more peaceful, she watched as Jack ran a lean, well-manicured hand down his mouth, thinking. It was a good mouth.

And it was a talented hand. *Stop it, Munie.* "OK I got one. What was your first arena concert?"

She laughed out loud. "Depeche Mode!"

He giggled, then began to look slightly uncomfortable, which made Munie grin broadly. "Oh boy, methinks this is going to be good. Dish, Coltrane."

"Does my family band count?"

"Absolutely not."

"Shit. OK." He sighed and rubbed at his forehead. "In that case, it was N'Sync. Right after I moved to the States."

As hard as she tried, Munie could not keep her mouthful of root beer in check this time, and her sip burst into the air in a shower of droplets. "I'm sorry—I don't mean to laugh."

"Yes you do." He just grinned good-naturedly, handing her a stack of napkins from the dispenser.

"It's just that I didn't expect you to be an N'Sync guy. I thought you were a jazz guy."

He grinned and lifted an eyebrow. "But she was an N-Sync girl."

"Ah. Priorities. Music is a powerful tool for love. How'd that work out for ya?" She chuckled and took a bite of her pizza, while he turned to look at her, a sly smile on his face and a twinkle in his eye.

"It was delicious." He winked and turned forward again.

She watched him lift his beer and take a long swig, studied the way his throat worked as he swallowed and the shape of his lips as they kissed the round opening of the bottle. Munie didn't have the capacity for a relationship in her life, not when her career was just starting sail on its own tailwind. And she had entirely too much self-respect to consider a partnership with someone who didn't even remember having slept with her in the first place. But that chemical attraction still pulled at her like a magnet. She remembered all too well the taste of his mouth, the flow and stroke of his hips, the indescribable way he could make her body feel.

And it had been a long time. She'd been so focused on work that she'd let any sort of intimate life languish for far too long. Yes, she's had lovers since that volcanic day with Jack four years ago, but a few seconds of mental math reconfirmed that there'd been no man at all in her bed for... a year? A year and a half? In any case, it had been a while.

As she watched Jack in profile, she realized just how much she was aching for that physical connection. And she knew down deep that she didn't want it with just anyone—she wanted it with him. She knew how incredible it felt, remembered how powerful their attraction was, could already feel the familiar tug of potent magnetism between them. Even if she didn't trust him, had no interest in a tomorrow with him, she realized she wanted that same heat, that alchemy, today, on her terms. So she decided to take it.

Munie laid down the gauntlet with her next question. "First song you ever had sex to."

His expression changed just slightly, becoming a little more aware, attuned—she watched his proverbial ears perk up. With no hesitation, he looked her squarely in the eye and replied, "'When Doves Cry.' You?"

This is when impulsiveness ultimately biffs you over the head, she immediately realized. She could lie— but no. Better to just take a breath and get it over with. Scrunching up her face and squeezing closed her eyes as if trying not see her own answer, she fessed up. "'Woman.'" *At least it wasn't "Jingle Bells,"* she thought to herself.

"'Woman'... by John Lennon?"

"Uh huh." Scrunching and squeezing were not proving to be nearly enough, so she covered her whole face with her hands, ruing the moment she chose this question in the first place. She blamed his cologne. And his neck. And his mouth. And his...

"The song where he apologizes for cheating on Yoko?" His voice went up half an octave on the last "o" in Yoko, as if he were trying not to laugh as he said it. Asshole.

She nodded from behind her hands. "Yup. Super sexy choice, I realize."

She heard him giggle, an airy and infectious sound, then felt his fingers gently guiding her hands from her face. His touch sent her pulse racing, and his proximity to her made her hungry for something much different than pizza.

"Hold up. Sauce." He brought his thumb to the corner of her mouth to wipe off a dot of marinara, and she watched as he slipped that thumb into his mouth and licked it clean, his eyes never moving from hers. Erotic memories flew through her head, and she was suddenly throbbing down low with the brazen want of him.

His voice came to her more softly this time, like a spell unfolding. "Here's a chance for redemption. What's the most *recent* song you had sex to?" He was clearly flirting with her now, and she was glad.

"I don't remember. It was over a year ago."

"What?"

"You heard me." Her tone was calm, direct, matter-of-fact. "What about you?"

He kept his eyes fixed on her. "My own song, sometime during the last tour, which ended five months ago."

"No girlfriend?"

"No. No boyfriend? No husband?"

She shook her head silently from side to side. He watched the movement, then drew his gaze down to her mouth and licked his lips. The ache at her center just grew louder in response.

She looked around surreptitiously to make sure they were still the only ones in the area, then leaned forward and grasped the shoulder of his shirt, bringing him close.

"This OK?" she whispered into his waiting mouth.

"Absolutely."

Munie was hungrier for that mouth than she had been for her food, and kissed him the same way she'd eaten—lustily, filling every corner of her tongue with him and savoring every morsel. Shit, he tasted good. And when he took her lower lip between his teeth and pulled, groaning as he did it, she knew he was just as hungry for her as she was for him.

Their foreheads touching, his thumb following the contours of her lips, he whispered, "Your hotel or mine?"

"My hotel. Your driver."

"Let's go."

Munie was absolutely not going to be one of those people who make out openly in the back seat of a car, so she just sat there, feeling Jack's thumb circle the inside of her palm and considering all the wickedness that would transpire once they closed her hotel room door. Given the silence on the other side of the seat, she was a thousand percent sure he was thinking along the same lines. She was also a thousand percent sure he was avoiding eye contact for the same reason she was. If they connected, even at that level, it was going to go down in this town car.

The hotel elevator was no better. For one thing, Jack had to face the back in order to avoid being recognized, with Munie directly in front of him, so that they were right in each other's frenetic space. Then, when they were finally alone again (why did she have to love high floors so much?), the old-school machinery just petered along at a painfully slow pace. But she wasn't a "Love in an Elevator" type either, so she just stood still across the car from him and watched the numbers. Ten floors to go.

Of course there was music piping through. And of course the next song to play was precisely the last one she wanted to hear. They tensed up in unison when they heard those first four immediately recognizable guitar plinks of supplication—"wah, wah, wah, WAH." And of course, Jack felt the need to start singing along with Marvin Gaye. Oh hell, he sounded good.

Seven floors to go. The gravelly growl in his voice hit her deep down. He was looking at her now as he continued to serenade her. Shit. Five floors. She could barely stay away when he sang those four self-manifesting words in the title: *Let's Get It On.*

He even did the wail, walking slowly to her side of the car as he crooned. Fortunately, just before Jack and Marvin were about to head into the second verse, perhaps making her a liar about the whole 'Love in an Elevator' thing, the doors dinged open and she bee-lined it down the corridor.

He grabbed her ass as she walked through the door, and she closed it with his body. They flung their jackets away with warp speed, and he immediately had both of her breasts in his grasp over her tee shirt, her hand cupping the utter hardness of his crotch. Then there was the sound of shoes slamming into things as they were wantonly kicked off. He pulled down her zipper while she pulled up his shirt to lick his chest from navel to nipples, spending a few extra seconds on that familiar music staff tattoo.

"Fuck." He growled into her neck as his hand dipped greedily inside her jeans, looking for the wet pool that waited for him. When he found it, he plunged deep with two fingers, making her moan loudly. "Oh fuck, Glenys."

She was too far gone to even laugh. His fingers dove into her again and again, his thumb circling her clit, while his mouth feasted upon her now naked breast. He used his other hand to help her undo his jeans, both of them jostling impatiently until she finally had her hand around the warm hardness of him. He was thick, sturdy, and desperately aroused. The carnal groan he gave her when she squeezed sent her immediately over the edge with a loud cry, as he continued to thrust his hand into her unabated. When he brought those fingers to his mouth, sucking them dry, she swooned.

"Your turn," she panted, simultaneously tugging at his jeans and pulling him toward an old oak desk next to the bed. With him behind her, his hand back in her pants, tongue at her neck, she worked to focus only long enough to find the condoms in the bottom of her overnight bag and rip one open. Turning back around to face him, she pushed her jeans down and off, sat on the desk, and shoved down his pants just far enough, rolling the latex onto his firm length as they both watched. They continued to watch as he slid into her with one long, deliberate thrust, trumping any memory she had of this sensation, then watched their bodies keep coming together over and over again in a demanding rhythm, his talented hips changing speed, force, and direction to make it exactly what she needed with each stroke. She watched him lick his thumb and bring it back to her nub, taking her just close enough, so that when he finally exploded with his deepest, most forceful thrust and a cry of her name, she was right there with him.

Three hours, two more condoms, several positions, and many delicious mouthfuls later, they tacitly agreed it was time for him to go. He left her in bed with a sweet kiss to the left cheek of her face and a deeply-drawn hickey to the right cheek of her buttocks. She fell asleep as the door clicked shut.

Songs on This Track

Superstar: Songwriters Bonnie Bramlett and Leon Russell; performed by Luther Vandross

A Case of You: Songwriter Joni Mitchell; performed by Prince

When Doves Cry: Lyrics and music by Prince; performed by Prince

Woman: Lyrics and music by John Lennon; performed by John Lennon

Love in an Elevator: Songwriters Joe Perry and Steven Tyler; performed by Aerosmith

Let's Get It On: Songwriters Marvin Gaye and Ed Townsend; performed by Marvin Gaye

6

LOVE IN THIS CLUB

July 2016
Las Vegas, NV

"Oooh, I think this is it."

The car rolled to a stop in front of the Castile Club on the Las Vegas Strip, a slightly drab, nondescript stone building set against a sidewalk teeming with loud, boisterous humanity.

"Do we really need to exit?" came the whine-in-brogue from the back seat, where Glenys was peering out the window with thinly veiled horror. "Someone could just spontaneously vomit on their shoes at any given moment."

Munie rolled her eyes and chuckled. "You'll like it better when we're inside, I promise. The day spa wasn't so bad, was it?"

"It was brilliant, but it was also in the light of day. No vampires were present during my body scrub, I'm quite certain, but this..."

"...will be epic. Come on."

The duo clambered out of the car and pushed through the throng into the building, which happily, was much less the chaotic party scene and more the top-shelf music venue that it was. Munie directed them toward a young man standing in the doorway in a crisp white dress shirt, tailored vest and dress pants, a serene smile aimed in their direction.

"Hello, hello!" she sang out, kissing him on both cheeks. "Micah, please meet my best friend, Glenys. Glen, this is Micah St. Jacques. He's just come on board with *Lift* as a project manager and I'm insanely lucky to have him on my team and as a friend." Micah just tilted his head demurely and smiled again, then took Glenys' hand in a gentle shake.

"Lovely to meet you, Micah. Any friend of Munie's, and all that. How are you finding the magazine so far? Rife with celebrity intrigue?"

He tilted his head again and gave a subtle wave of his hand. "Oh honey, it does have its moments, doesn't it? But I've got Munie, so I'm always good. And she's got me. We're gonna take care of each other. And isn't that what it's all about when you get right down to it?" His accent was decidedly Southern and his delivery delicious.

"Hear hear! Oh darling, I do believe we're going to be forever friends. Let's get started immediately!" She grabbed Micah by one elbow, Munie took his other one with a giggle, and the three of them made their way into the heart of the building.

It was a stunning venue—new everything, with shiny oak floors, beautiful furnishings, and a giant modern art mosaic chandelier to die for. Just class on class on class. "Now this I could warm up to," Glenys cooed as Micah distributed their tickets. "Thank you kindly, love. Mun, how did you say this came about again?"

"It was all Micah's doing," Munie nodded with a smile in his direction. "I've interviewed Nickles Boone a couple of times over the years—he owns this club. Micah reached out to him, told him we were visiting, and cha-ching! Magic tickets!"

"Brilliant. And who are we to be seeing tonight, then—oh gosh, no way! Tiyani Keith?!"

"One woman show! We thought you'd love it. Happy Birthday, Glen!"

"Fucking tossers," Glenys replied, wiping at her eyes.

"You're welcome," Munie smiled back, folding her best friend in her arms. "I love you." As the lights flickered and the chimes sounded, they made their way to their seats, arms linked.

Two hours and twenty minutes later, the trio emerged into the lobby once again, squinting, smiling and giddy with satisfaction.

"That was bloody brilliant."

"Couldn't have said it better."

"Now where's the bar?" Glenys scanned around, spotted her destination, and began walking.

"Not so fast," Munie laughed, placing herself between the birthday girl and the the gorgeous polished oak bar on the other side of the room. "Micah and I have one more birthday trick up our sleeves. Walk this way."

The two women followed their speed walking guide through rivulets of posh, delicately-scented concert-goers, out a back door of the main venue into a corridor, through that into another large open space, up an escalator and into a red-roped queue around the corner.

"Where on Earth, Munie?" Glenys had stopped to lean against a column and massage what was likely a well-blistered foot.

"Worth it, Glen, I promise."

Once it was their turn in line, Micah said a few magic words to the gentlemen at the door, and their little party was promptly hand-stamped and welcomed through.

The room beyond the door was frantic—dark, loud, and crowded—with a live DJ in the corner, a crammed-to-the-gills dance floor in front of it, and a series of lounging couches and low tables lined throughout the rest of the space. You couldn't hear yourself scream.

"Wait!" Munie yelled and mimed simultaneously, pointing at a second room. "Let's go out there." She grabbed Micah's hand, he grabbed Glenys' hand, and the three of them snaked their human chain through the web of bodies and onto a patio bearing more lounges but less noise, plus a welcome wash of fresh night air.

Once again stationary, Munie and Micah held a silent look-and-gesture game until Micah finally indicated a sofa and table in the corner near the balcony.

"Ready?" Munie beamed to a thoroughly befuddled Glenys, who just shook her head and laughed.

"I've no fucking idea, ducks, but why not go for it? Drive on!" Once they reached their destination, however, Glenys was utterly lost for words.

"Glenys MacKenzie, please meet Tiyani Keith. Tiyani, this is Glenys."

"My pleasure, and a Happy Birthday to you," cooed the beautiful woman with creamy ebony skin and the graceful gestures of a ballet dancer.

Munie savored every second of the next fifteen minutes as she watched Glenys' utter delight at sipping prosecco in the warm night air with her favorite vocalist, talking and laughing like the new friends they were becoming.

The five minutes that followed that, however, could rank up there with very few other interactions that Munie wanted to immediately forget ever took place.

"Is that Rai Paley I see?"

Nickles Boone was standing beside her all of a sudden, grinning ear to ear, and making her heart swell in parallel.

"Nickles! How long has it been?!" She popped up from her seat to receive a kiss on both cheeks. "Almost ten years now, right?"

"I think that's it, girl. You look fantastic. And you're doing great out there. I'm real proud of you."

She had to look down to the street below for a second in order to rein in control of the emotion just pricking behind her eyes. Fortunately, Nickles had moved along to Tiyani, congratulating her on a beautiful show. Munie reset and found his gaze again.

"Thank you," she smiled back, "and thank you so much for all of this. Please meet my best friend, Glenys. Today is her birthday."

"Well Happy Birthday, baby girl!" he called out exuberantly. "Is it happy?"

"So happy," Glenys beamed, extending her hand only to be pulled into a bear hug and kissed loudly on both cheeks.

"Bo, where you at?" came a holler from halfway across the patio.

As boisterous as it was, there was a familiar note in that voice that struck Munie's ear.

"Aw shit," Nickles muttered under his breath, then, more loudly as he waved his arm in the direction of the hollerer, "Over here!" Five seconds later, their little group had grown by three members, one of whom made Munie's stomach drop to the floor. Jack. Again. But the man standing before her bore very little resemblance to the versions she remembered from any of their past interactions.

Even though he was shorter than Nickles by a good margin—maybe about 5′7″ if Munie had to guess—he somehow took up the whole space. He looked like the definition of Las Vegas, decked out in bell-bottom belted pants, shiny white dress shoes, a silk shirt open at the chest, Rolex and chains, and a drink in his hand to complete the picture. It was a far cry from the flannel, tee shirt, or sweater and jeans version of Jack she knew, and she wasn't warming up to this new model one little bit.

"Where the fuck did you go, man?" He was waving his arms at Nickles now, and talking a little more loudly than necessary.

"Tryna get away from your ass," Nickles quipped with a half-smile. "Folks, may I introduce Gene Coltrane. Gene, this is Rai Paley, Micah St. Jacques, and Glenys."

His gaze traveled across the group, then settled quickly back on Munie. Shit. She held her breath, hoping this didn't go sideways in one of many possible ways. "Rai," he echoed, like he was tasting the word. "You kinda hot, Rai." His eyes were crawling up and down her body in the most uncomfortable of ways, roving from breasts to belly to buttocks and around again. When they finally landed on her face, though, two facts became abundantly clear: 1. Jack was high as a kite; and 2. he didn't remember Munie at all.

"Maybe we can get together later on to see the city lights or something," he drawled. His smile would have been beautiful if it weren't so lecherous. "Jimmy, help her out, man."

The gentleman to Gene's left pulled out what looked like a calling card and held it out to her. Dumbstruck at his utter audacity, she took it only because she had no earthly idea what else to do.

"Gene baby, let's get you some water or something." Nickles had placed his large hand on Jack's shoulder and was not-so-gently guiding him away from the scene. As he did, he looked over his own shoulder to address the trio of friends, managing a warm smile atop simmering anger. "Micah, Rai, so good to see you both again. And Glenys, have a blessed birthday."

Almost so as not to let the encounter end on a good note, Jack turned around as well to throw an additional flaming bag of feces onto the fire. "Call me, Rai baby—we'll get it on real good. Maybe we could even '*Make Love in this Club.*'"

All Munie could do was stare open-mouthed as the group of men retreated, Nickles now holding the still-singing Jack in what was almost a half-nelson. Flabbergasted, she turned back to the couch to sit down and collect her thoughts, only to discover that Tiyani had ducked away sometime after the arrival of Jack and his crew.

"Shit!" She flopped down on the sofa and put her head in her hands. This entire situation was so bizarre.

She felt Glenys come to rest beside her and place a soothing hand on her shoulder. She spoke in a quiet, gentle tone. "Are you OK? That Gene arsehole was downright abusive."

"Oh, I'm fine, really. Not the first drugged-up 'arsehole' I've met by any means. I'm just pissed he drove Tiyani away." And she was pissed that he didn't remember her, and pissed that the sweet, sincere man she once knew had devolved into the caricature she'd just observed. "Do you want to find her? Maybe—"

"No, love," Glenys interrupted, hands in front of her like a subtle stop sign. "It's been a magical birthday, but I am completely and utterly knackered, and I would love to get back to the hotel before my feet swell permanently into these pumps."

Munie smiled in spite of herself. The fancy spa bathrobe waiting in her room did sound amazing. "Excellent idea, ducks! Shall we?" she offered, standing and extending her hand.

There was a tiny wood-burning fireplace on the ground floor of the building, and as they walked past it on the way out, Munie flicked Gene Coltrane's card into the middle of the flames. "Micah, let's keep him off the interview list," she said with a sigh and a slow, sad shake of her head.

Songs **on this Track**

Love in this Club: Songwriters Usher Raymond, Polow da Don, Young Jeezy, Lamar Taylor, Ryon Lovett, Keith Thomas, Darnell Dalton; performed by Usher

7

LOVE ME IN A SPECIAL WAY

November 2018
Los Angeles, CA

"The word 'tartare' doesn't sound as though it should be a food, really."

"Then what should it be?"

Glenys plopped her menu onto the table and pursed her lips, looking skyward. "It sounds like a word of soothing, somehow. As in, 'Oh blast, my boyfriend and I broke up.' 'Well, tartare, love, there are bigger fish in the sea.'"

Munie laughed out loud. "She's gonna love you."

Glenys' eyes twinkled as she sipped her second mimosa. "Don't they all, then?"

"Of course."

Munie wished they could be roommates all the time. It was so perfect, so wonderful to have her best friend here in LA to share her down time with, rather than via smartphone as usual. But unfortunately, Glenys and Munie had to cram all their in-person catch ups into three or four week or long-weekend stints across the year, since neither of their schedules permitted anything longer or more frequent. That would be increasingly true now, Munie mused with a little thrill she couldn't stifle.

As if on cue, two familiar faces popped up beside the table.

"Perfect timing!" Munie hopped up to kiss and hug Micah as well as the short, curvy woman next to him. "I'm so happy we could make this happen."

"Micah! Bring it in, darling!" Glenys boomed, jumping out of her seat to wrap him in a rugby-caliber hug. "My goodness, you're a sight for sore eyes. What's it been, almost a whole year now, yeah?"

"That's it," Micah replied smoothly. "And not for nothing, day drinking with you at the Kentucky Derby is an experience I went ahead and socked away to remember in all future situations for which a little mood boost is required."

"Oh, I want in next time!" This from the woman next to Micah.

Munie giggled. "It's a party, then. Glenys, please meet Latisha Singh. She's the senior client and talent partner at *Lift*. And apparently, your next date for the Derby."

"Brilliant to meet you, Latisha. If experience speaks, we're destined to be close chums by the end of this luncheon. Mun's work family has been a divine cast of characters thus far."

Latisha smiled as she took her seat. "Rai here is a total rock star." Turning her focus to Munie, she continued. "Girl, you do realize this promotion is about two years overdue, right?"

Munie just grinned. "Better late than never, I guess. I'm just happy I'm not STILL an accountant."

"Bloody well right!" came the response from the slightly champagne-laced Scottish corner of the table. The whole group erupted in laughter, Latisha yelling "OK I'm keepin' you, Glenys!" as the two women clinked glasses.

Micah, who was apparently the excitability antithesis of Latisha, merely leaned forward over his interlaced hands, a polite smile on his face. "So how long do we have you in town this time around, Glenys darlin'?"

"Just for a few days. Then we head up into Vancouver for a week —late birthday trip for Mun. I'll fly back to the UK from there."

"Sounds lovely."

"'Tis. What more could a girl ask for, eh?"

"Nothing, as long as she's got her Happy Stash," Munie chimed in with a giggle.

Glenys guffawed in response. "Too right."

Latisha raised an eyebrow. "What kind of stash are we talking about here, girl?"

Glenys tutted and gave a dismissive wave. "Oh please. Even in sex dreams, I'm not that exciting." She pulled up a large canvas handbag from the floor and placed it in her lap. "Have a look. Everywhere I go—and my partner is a pilot with British Airways, so I go a lot—I'm never without my personal collection of home comforts."

"Come on, then," Latisha laughed. "What you got in there?"

Munie pinched the space between her eyebrows as Glenys dove in Mary Poppins-style with one hand. "Are you seriously going to empty that thing in here?"

"Munie love, I have a rapt audience intent on learning my tricks of the trade. How could I let them down?" She cleared away the empty plate and silverware from the space in front of her in order to make more room.

"Now then. Since most of the tea you have here in America (and in many other places) is right sock water, I always carry my own." She plopped a canister of loose oolong onto the table, along with a metal tea ball, and followed that with a small medicine bottle. "Next, paracetamol. If it works, it works, eh Micah?"

"Yes ma'am," he concurred smoothly, gesturing with one hand for emphasis.

"The smaller bits I won't pull out—favorite sweets, warm socks, massage balls—"

"What?" Latisha was laughing and intrigued in equal measure.

"No judging until you've tried them, love, and once you do, Bob's your uncle if you're not carrying a pair in that little Gucci purse of yours at all times." She kept rummaging. "What else? Ah yes. Can't be without these."

Reaching in deeply once again, she retrieved both an e-reader and a small stack of periodicals.

"Oh no. Is that *OK Magazine*? I love *OK!*" Micah reached out eagerly, and Glenys thrust a copy into his hand.

"Absolutely. None of that American rubbish for me—present company excluded, of course. British rubbish only!" She laughed heartily and passed issues to both Munie and Latisha.

The four lunch mates spent the next thirty minutes eating fancy canapes, drinking mimosas, and thumbing through the full stack of magazines. Given the career profile of most of the table, it was a singular experience.

"Oh she is a trip, this one," Latisha offered, turning around her copy so that everyone could see the image on the page. "She once left a restaurant after a $300 meal without tipping because the server gave her sweet tea versus unsweetened tea."

"Where did you hear that?" Glenys asked, wide-eyed.

"I was with her. After her car came, I hauled ass back inside before all hell broke loose to put down my company card." She closed the magazine, grabbed another issue from the pile, and pointed at the cover. "But this dude, on the other hand, is the real deal. Six-foot-five and looks like a Greek god, but he's a total teddy bear."

"Wouldn't mind snuggling up with him at night, hey?" Glenys quipped.

"Preach," agreed Micah, peeking from behind his copy. "Oh and here's a live one. Remember him?" he said as he tilted the page toward Glenys.

"Ah, the arsehole. That was quite a night, wasn't it? Do you recall, Mun? He virtually ravished you with his eyes, after all. So bizarre. What's the name again there, Micah?"

"Gene Coltrane."

Munie choked on her iced tea. Before she could recover and make words, though, Latisha was on the scene.

"Oh yeah, Mr. Swag Bag himself. What happened?"

Micah placed the open magazine on the table and folded his

hands. "He basically accosted Rai a couple of years ago in Vegas. Out of his mind high. It was embarrassing."

He sighed. "And sad. You know, back when I was in college, he spoke at a creative arts event on campus. This was probably my junior year, so 2004, let's say. He was just starting out—it was him and his writing partners." He looked down at the picture, then back up at the group. "He was so sweet and so genuine. I remember thinking what a great person he was." He sighed again and picked up a canape. "It's sad what fame can do."

"I think he's coming out of it, though," Latisha said as she poured another mimosa. "He's just about to release another album, which—blessed be—isn't more of that lame R&B shit he's been doing lately—although the cover he did of 'Love Me in a Special Way' last year is still on my playlist. Anyway, he's back to jazz now, and my people tell me it's absolute fire. Plus he's clean and sober again."

Munie's heart swelled. Regardless of how Jack remembered her (or not), she thought of him with kilograms of tenderness, and to hear that he was perhaps coming closer to the Jack she once knew was like a dollop of balm applied to an aching wound. She was too rife with emotion to speak, and happy she didn't need to say anything at the moment.

"Is he doing the circuits?" Micah asked. He and Latisha were eye to eye now, zeroing in for shop talk.

"He's about to. As a matter of fact, I've been thinking about setting up an interview with him for *Lift*. May take a while to get it on the books if he heads out on tour for this record, but could be a good full-circle moment. But only with someone who could break that infuriating habit he has of not talking about his personal life."

Micah caught Munie's gaze across the table, and she could read his expression clear as day. She knew what he was thinking. She was one of the best journalists out there when it came to getting interviewees to open up, so she'd be top of the list for working with someone as enigmatic as Gene Coltrane. She also knew, for all the reasons that weren't known around the table, that what he was considering would be a beehive of emotion for her. But on the other hand, it could also be a way to finally close out this odd Jack Flores chapter of her life—to decode, classify, and file it away once and for all. For that reason, interviewing Jack was a challenge worth considering, and so even if it still required a lot of thought, she was at least ready to hear Micah's question when he asked it out loud.

"Should we put him back on the interview list, honey?"

Songs on this Track

Love Me in a Special Way: Songwriter El DeBarge; performed by DeBarge

PART II

IN YOUR EYES

8

———————

PRE-SESSION

How's it going there, Micah?

> This suite is incredible. Top floor, view of the mountains, and there's even an Italian portico on the other side for their lunch. Nicely done, Latisha.

Anything for you, honey. What's the setup inside?

> I'm around the corner in the kitchen with Ethan.

?

> Coltrane's assistant.

Ah.

> Rai's going to record on her end and we'll be listening in on headphones out of view. She wanted a "closed set." They'll be in the giant drawing room in these fancy-ass chairs that Elizabeth I probably sat in.

Yeah, she likes a closed set. Wait up—what do you mean "will be"? This thing was supposed to start at 9 am.

Coltrane's not here yet.

It's almost ten! WTF?

Ethan says he's on his way. I don't know anything more than that. Rai's ready.

Just one little wrinkle.

Tell me.

She hasn't had any coffee yet.

Oh shit.

I know.

Here he comes.

Keep me posted.

9

WHAT YOU WON'T DO FOR LOVE

GENE COLTRANE INTERVIEW, OCTOBER 21, 2019

The Bellweather Hotel, Studio City, CA
Audio Recording Part 1

"So how's this gonna go?"

"I don't know. You tell me."

"I'm a little scared—not gonna lie. I've heard you make your men cry."

"Only because they're sad when it's over."

(He bursts into surprised laughter.) "So I'm gonna spill my guts, tell you all my darkest shit, and cry when it's over, huh?"

"Wouldn't be the first time, Gene."

(A long pause.) "Let's go."

"Just for the record, please state your name and today's date."

"Gene Coltrane. October 21, 2019."

"And I'm Rai Paley, interviewing for *Lift* magazine."

"Ray, like in Ray Charles?"

"No, Rai like in the Sanskrit."

"What's it mean?"

"Tell you after the interview."

"Shit."

"Them's the breaks. You're the star; you get the questions."

"You're a real ray of sunshine."

"That's what they all say. Tell me about your first kiss."

"What?"

"Tell me about your first kiss. Easy question. And remember—I'm only recording to take notes later—you get to approve this whole thing before it goes to print, so don't trip."

"But how is that an interview question?"

"It's an icebreaker."

"OK, then tell me about yours first."

"What?"

"You heard me. You go first."

"Why would I do that? It's my interview."

(A pause, followed by the creak of a chair.) "Because this here is a two-person situation. You want something personal from me, you got to give me something personal back in return. Lawyers call that something, don't they?"

"Quid pro quo."

"That's it. *Quid pro quo.* You 'pro' and I 'quo.' And that's the way it goes." *(He chuckles; another creak.)* "First kiss."

(A long pause; she sighs.) "OK, fine. He was a trumpet player in the high school band. It was in his backyard as we were walking home from a date. In the moonlight. It was perfect, and he was an excellent, top-shelf kisser. So there you go."

"Tongue?"

"No. Why?"

"Context. Sometimes it goes there."

"Your turn. Wait—before we start, I need to ask you for a favor. Could you please take off your shades?"

"Huh?"

"I'd like to be able to see your eyes. It's important for a conversation like this—helps me to get to know you a little."

"Yeah, fine, OK." *(The click of earpieces folding together, and the soft thump of an item being placed on a table. A few moments of heavy silence ensue, followed by the clearing of throats and rustling of papers.)*

"Thanks a lot—much better. So now, first kiss…"

"My friend's sister. In the den. We were watching a movie, he left to go to the bathroom or something, and we just kind of leaned into each other, then Bam!"

"Tongue?"

"No! I was twelve."

(She laughs.)

"How old were you, anyway?"

"Sixteen."

"Damn! That's like a book or something—*Bob and Jane Kiss in the Moonlight.*"

"You're a card."

"Jack of diamonds, baby."

"You have a beautiful smile."

"Thanks." (*He laughs.*) "Caps are a wonderful thing."

"Ha! At least you avoided braces."

"Not really. I needed braces growing up, but by the time I was in high school, we couldn't afford it, so I got caps as soon as I made some decent money writing."

"And that lean time came about when your dad split, right? I did some reading up, but keep me honest on all of this."

"*They* split. My dad didn't take off."

"OK. But after the divorce, your father went on the road and left you and your sisters with an uncle, is that right?"

"No, it was me and my brother. My sisters stayed with my mom." (*A pause.*) "Oh shit, this is a great song. Know the title? Three seconds—think fast." (*Another pause.*) "Time's up." (*Sings.*) "*What You Won't Do for Love.*"

"Gene?"

"Bobby Caldwell. That's a classic right there."

(She calls out in a slightly louder voice.) "Micah? Could you please turn down the music piping in here? Thank you."

"Damn. You're stone cold."

"So I've heard. Back to your parents, and thank you for the clarification. How often was your dad home, then?"

(*He sighs.*) "Once a month, maybe? Something like that. I don't remember the exact cadence."

"And during that time you played sax in your uncle's jazz band?"

"Right."

"You were how old?"

"Sixteen, seventeen."

"Did you see your mom and sisters a lot?"

"Yeah, a few times a week. She made sure." (*A pause*). "That's a cool anklet."

"Thanks. What made you decide to switch to vocals?"

"Money."

(*She laughs*).

"No. Seriously, I just started to not love it so much, know what I mean? Playing sax all the time was getting a little stale, and I didn't like how that felt. So, I changed things up. Plus, I wanted to sing more."

"Lucky us."

(*His voice is warm.*) "Thanks."

(*The clink of glass, and the thunk of something heavy being placed on a table.*) "Ah, thank you!" (*The sound of pouring, sipping, and the plink of a cup in a saucer.*) "Coffee is truly the nectar of the gods."

(*His laugh, followed by more sipping.*)

"What comes first, Gene, music or lyrics?"

"Depends."

"On what?"

"My mood. Where I'm at. Who I'm with."

"Who were you with when you wrote 'Green?'"

"No one. I was alone in a hotel room in Memphis or Cleveland or something. Don't remember. The riff just came in and I wrote around that."

"How long did it take?"

"To finish?"

"Yeah."

"Three, four hours. Three bourbons and about half a dozen smokes."

"How did you start smoking?"

"Like a lot of kids. School."

"Why?"

"I don't know—I guess to look cool. Then because it felt good."

"How much do you smoke? Your friends do call you 'Chimney,' right?"

(*He laughs out loud.*) "Now how do you know about that?"

"I have my ways."

(*A chair creaks; his voice becomes conspiratorial.*) "But is that really why they call me that?"

(*She speaks the same way.*) "Why else?"

"Maybe it has to do with my big chute."

(*She laughs out loud—a throaty belly laugh.*)

(*A pause. His voice is husky.*) "Baby, I love that laugh."

"It's Rai."

"Sorry. Rai."

"It's OK… Gene. Why'd you pick Gene?"

"As a stage name?"

"Yes."

"Because of Gene Kelly."

"No way!"

"One hundred percent."

(*A pause, then more clinking and sipping, followed by the sound of the cup and saucer being placed on a table.*)

"Let's go back to your move to LA. You were nineteen when you came to the States, right?"

"Yeah. You've been reading up, I see."

(*She sighs.*) "Something like that."

"The first place I lived wasn't actually in LA, though. My buddy Lark and I got a tiny little—I guess a bungalow?—in this town called Via Clara."

(*A pause; her voice becomes quiet.*) "I know Via Clara well."

(*Another pause; his tone matches hers.*) "Do you, Rai?"

"Yeah." (*She clears her throat; her delivery becomes more polished.*) "But that's kind of far from LA, isn't it?"

"Oh yeah—it was a pain in the ass. But we got a deal on the place, some family friend of his, and two young, poor horn players, so..."

"Oh you mean Lark Benson!"

"Yeah, yeah." (*His tone is wistful.*) "We had a blast."

"I'm sorry. Such a terrible loss for the jazz community. He was a gifted young man."

"Yeah... he was."

"But have you heard that Lark House raised three million dollars for inner-city drug awareness and rehabilitation just last year? That's a wonderful legacy."

"Yeah."

(*A chair creaks; she changes the tone of her voice.*) "So then, when did you move to LA?"

(*Another silent beat, then he brightens.*) "Not until I sold my first album as an artist. It wasn't released—hell it wasn't even made!—but I had the forward for it, and a good few production royalties stacked up by that point." (*He laughs quietly.*) "It was this fine-looking two-story chalet-style thing out in Laurel Canyon. All these complicated fixtures and designs. And I didn't know what the hell to put in there! You know, it came with these huge old bookshelves, and I think the only thing I ever put on there was my wallet."

(*Silence.*)

"What? You run out of questions already, Ms. Interviewer?"

(*Her single, protracted chuckle.*) "Not even close. Sorry—that just made me think of something. Keep going."

"My sisters kept telling me I needed an interior designer. That's not me. Anyway." (*Pouring; ice clinking.*) "Your turn."

"OK, then. What you got?"

"What's your whole name?"

"Raimunda. Raimunda Penelope Paley."

"Damn!"

"Yep. Your turn. Full name, please."

"You already know what it is."

"For the record."

"Jackson Martinez Kensington Flores."

"Now that's a name."

"Damn straight."

"Cuban dad, Bahamian mom, right?"

"Correct."

"Raised in the Bahamas, correct?"

"Correct."

"Mom was an opera singer?"

"Yes ma'am. The best. And Daddy was a music man."

"Five of you kids?"

"Yes."

(*She pauses.*) "And how many do you have?"

(*Sipping and ice clinking as he responds.*) "How many what?"

"Kids."

(*A long beat of silence*). "What the hell?"

"Be honest, Gene. The tabs are all over the place on this. It's been THE hot info leak over the last two weeks. You diddled around the world on tour for a decade, slipping it anywhere you wanted. One mother came forward three years ago claiming you're the daddy, then another, and another, and now you've got a whole soccer team. Good luck trying to keep something like that private when you're a celebrity like Gene Coltrane, right?"

(*The loud thud of a glass on a table, the dragging of chair legs, microphone interference, and footsteps. His voice comes as a shout, further away from the microphone.*) "Fuck this! Fuck you, Rai. I'm done. Ethan, get this fucking mike off me right now."

(*A sip and a clink.*) "You do realize that you get to approve this content, right? You don't want it public, it doesn't go public."

(*He's loud, agitated, his voice pitched high.*) "Then why in the fuck would you even ask me?"

(*Her tone remains calm and professional.*) "Two reasons. One—if this story really is true, you might just want a solid, respected place like *Lift* in which to go public." (*More sipping and clinking.*) "And two—now we have a real interview. Pleasure to meet you, Gene. Is that what everyone who really knows you calls you?"

(*A long beat of silence, followed by a heavy sigh from a distance. Footsteps come slowly toward the mike; the sound of heavy sitting and another long pause. His voice is resigned and tired.*) "Jack. I'm Jack."

(*A pause. Her voice is warm and gentle.*) "Munie." (*A long silence.*) "Well, aren't you going to shake my hand, Jack? Don't leave me hanging here."

(*His deep exhale, the gentle groaning of chairs, then two abrupt intakes of breath, followed by a heavy silence. He clears his throat; his tone is vulnerable.*)

"Munie?"

"Yes?"

"That's your real name, right?"

"Yes, Jack."

(*Silence.*) "OK."

"Why?"

"Nothing." (*A long pause.*) "Four."

"What?"

"I got four kids. Two girls and two boys."

(*She exhales as if in a smile, her voice warm.*) "Thank you, Jack."

(*He chuckles airily.*) "Fuck you, Munie."

(*Playfully.*) "Wasn't that the issue in the first place?"

(*They're both silent for a second, then simultaneously burst into giggles. Sounds of talking grow in the background.*)

"Sorry Jack. One sec. What's up, Micah? Ohhhhh. Every twenty? Wow. OK, got it."

"What's going on? Something with the mike?"

"No, no. Apparently, your contract requires us to break every twenty minutes of the interview for a ten-minute period."

"What? I didn't ask for that."

"The label did."

"Shit. I'm sorry."

"It's OK. Really. Happens a fair bit."

"On twenty?"

"Well, no."

(They laugh in unison, then fall into a prolonged silence. Her voice is quiet and warm.) "See you in ten, Jack."

"I'll be here."

Songs on this Track

<u>*What You Won't Do for Love:*</u> Songwriters Bobby Caldwell and Alfons Kettner; performed by Bobby Caldwell

10

SINGAPORE STREET

GENE COLTRANE INTERVIEW, OCTOBER 21, 2019

The Bellweather Hotel, Studio City, CA
Audio Recording Part 2

"LET'S SWITCH TOPICS, SHALL WE?"

"Yes fucking please."

"I'd like to go back to your time in Via Clara, if that's OK."

"You're the boss."

"You move out here, don't know anyone, don't know where your next paycheck will come from... just a lot of uncertainty."

"I was young." (*He chuckles.*)

"You still are."

"Nah. You age fast in this business."

"What's aged you?"

"Interviews like this!"

"Be serious. I want to know."

"I don't know—late nights, smog, being on the road, surer than shit... all the stuff that comes with it..."

"Such as?"

"Partying, never being in the same bed or the same city. Fast food. Can't work out."

"Do you work out normally?"

"No."

"OK then." (*Her tone becomes slightly softer.*) "What do you miss when you're on the road?"

"How do you mean?"

"Just that."

"I don't get it."

"What's not to get?"

"I love the road. The band, the diversity, the fact that every day is different. I love it all."

"Then what happens when you come home? What's your 'every day' off the road?"

(*Silence.*) "I honestly don't know."

"There must be something... a pet, a group of friends, pickle-ball..." (*He laughs.*) "What's at home, Jack?"

(*A long beat of silence.*) "Before the first album, there was Lark, my gigs, my day job, writing every day... all those things made up a community, I guess. I mean, it was a community of people scrounging to pull together pizza money, but still." (*She laughs.*) "I guess when I started touring in '08, all that fell back. I mean, Lark was..."

"Right..."

"...and my family was back home, so it was just... I guess... acquaintances. Everyone I really know well now is on the road with me." (*A lengthy silence, then he sighs.*) "I never really thought about it that way. I guess I don't have a lot at home right now." (*A pause; his voice is pensive.*) "Wow. That's heavy."

(*Silence; her tone becomes brighter.*) "My turn. Ask me something."

(*A pause; he responds with more liveliness.*) "Best vacation you ever had."

"Ooooh—good one!" (*Fingernails drumming against wood.*) "Probably Croatia, about eight years ago, I think?"

"Boyfriend?"

"Nope, best friend. Her name is Glenys—we were college room-mates. She's from Scotland but lives in London now."

"What made it the best?"

(*A pause.*) "I don't know how to answer that. It was just everything. Not the beaches or the food or the old towns—they were all amazing —but we went totally as just us, just being. At home during that time, there were all these opinions from other people about what I should do with my life, which decisions I should make, et cetera. But on our vacation, I had no one to be a certain way for, no expectations. We were free to just... do. Just be."

"Aren't you always?"

(*A pause.*) "I guess not."

(*His tone is deeper, softer.*) "Then who are you?"

(*Silence. She speaks quietly, as if to herself.*) "Maybe I'm still trying to figure that out, I suppose."

(*A chair creaks softly; his voice becomes more intimate*). "So when do you feel... you?"

(*Her tone is equally quiet.*) "When I'm doing this." (*A pause.*) "Like now. I feel me now."

(*His voice is almost a whisper.*) "That's good." (*Several seconds of silence, then an intake of breath.*)

(*She takes on a more professional tone.*) "Your turn. What happened to your eye?"

"This one?"

"Yep. Looks like you lost at least one round."

(*A long beat of silence.*) "Truth?"

"Always, Jack."

"It was Jennifer."

"Marini?"

"Yeah."

"Why would your girlfriend give you a shiner like that?"

(*The creak of a chair, followed by footsteps retreating and the sound of drapes being pulled.*)

"Take your time."

(*His voice comes from slightly further away. *) "We got about five minutes until the next break."

"Not important."

(*A full minute of silence. The sound of footsteps coming toward the mike again, and another chair creak. He sighs.*) "Jen always wanted kids. I wasn't ready, so we never tried until about a year ago. Nothing happened. Then she found out about the other kids."

"Ah."

"Yeah. And we've been together for five years, so you do the math. She was pissed."

"Are you?"

"What?"

"Pissed. At yourself."

(*He speaks quietly.*) "Yeah."

"Is it over?"

(*Sarcastically.*) "What do you think? That ain't a hickey."

"Did you love her?"

"No. Yes. Sort of." (*He exhales audibly.*) "I loved her like a ... like a work partner—like in an office—your work wife or work husband... like that."

"What about her?"

"Same. We even opened up the relationship, you know?"

"So why was she so angry?"

"Because I said no to kids with her, and we made sure we couldn't get pregnant, but..."

(*She sighs.*) "...it wasn't the same on the road."

"Right."

(*Sipping and clinking.*) "Have you ever been in love, Jack? Because you write and sing like you have."

(*His voice takes on a deeper tone.*) "Have you ever been in love, Munie?"

"How else would I have known to make the comment I just made? Stop deflecting and answer the question, please."

(*The creak of a chair; his voice is intimate.*) "Yes. Yes, I've been in love."

"With all those women?"

"No. Infatuated with all of them, yes. In love with all of them, no."

(*A pause.*) "I'm mortal, you know? I'm passionate. Sometimes I let that passion take over."

"In your life or in your writing?"

"Both. When I write, it makes for a great song. But in life, it makes for some 'heat of the moment' decisions that have longer-term consequences for people other than me."

"What happens after?"

"After?"

"After the infatuation ends."

(*He sighs.*) "After, I walk out the door and that's it. It goes from something I can't hardly manage in my heart to something I might write a song about. But, you know, I'm not pouring out 'When I Was Your Man' or some shit."

(*She laughs loudly.*) "Noted." (*A long pause.*) "And after you fall in love?"

(*His response is immediate.*) "I stay in love."

(*Heavy silence.*)

"These affairs don't last, they're hard on your heart, and they have obvious consequences, yet you keep going down that road. Why?"

(*Wistfully.*) "I guess I just like romance, infatuation. Love." (*A pause.*) "Hell Munie, I think it may be happening right now."

"But it'll end as soon as this interview does."

"Not if it's love." (*Several beats of heavy silence. She clears her throat. He chuckles deeply.*)

"Let's get specific on the musical side of this. I presume I know some of the songs resulting from your serial infatuations, right?"

(*His tone is playful, amused.*) "I'm sure you do."

"OK, how about..." (*A pause.*) "Oh! 'Baseline and Moment.'"

(*Dreamily.*) "Oh, yeah."

"So? Dish. I want to know."

(*He lets out a long, relaxed sigh.*) "Beautiful woman named Naomi. I met her at the Curaçao Jazz Festival. Background singer. Incredible voice." (*Warmly.*) "Damn."

"Go on."

"This was maybe 2007—even 2006—before most people knew my

face. We went out clubbing after our sets, since we both finished early in the evening. That whole night was magic—the jazz beats in the background, us dancing and talking around it, the breeze and the salt in the air. It was beautiful."

"Do you keep in touch?"

"No. Not after that night."

"Does she even know you wrote that song about her?"

"Dunno." *(The sound of hands drumming on thighs. His voice is merry and energetic.)* "Pick another one."

"OK... ah yes. I love this one. 'Singapore Street.'" *(She quotes from the song.)* "*'Gliding down a dark street in the warm rain, droplets dancing on my tongue...,'* that image of a couple sitting on a porch swing to keep out of the storm. It's just so evocative, so romantic. And the ballad itself is simply stunning from a musical perspective."

"Romantic, huh?"

"Absolutely. Well, you wrote it, Jack, you tell me. Tell me all about 'Singapore Street.'"

"It's about sex."

"Oh come on, be serious."

"One hundred percent. Singapore Street is a woman I met in Singapore, at a bar. The song is every inch about her body." *(His tone is low, flirty.)* "It's me on Singapore Street."

(Silence.)

(He sings.) "*'Sweet plum taste of summer on the soft sand'*... that's her mouth when I kissed her real deep."

(More silence. Her voice is quiet.) "The porch swing?"

(He chuckles deeply and sings again.) "*'Rocking, rocking, rocking on her porch swing, holding her eyes on mine.'* Rockin.'" *(The rhythmic creak of a chair and her sharp intake of breath.)*

"Oh shit. So the dark street... "

" ...is her pussy."

"And the warm rain..."

"Uh huh. *(He sings.)* *'With droplets dancing on my tongue.'* You get all that, Munie?"

· · ·

Songs on this Track

When I Was Your Man: Songwriters Bruno Mars, Philip Lawrence, Ari Levine, Andrew Wyatt; performed by Bruno Mars

11

BREAK #2

Sorry—the first break was busy. Second
break starting now.

Please tell me he's sober?

As a judge.

Thank God. So?

Our girl is a complete rock star, no pun
intended. He fessed up to the kid thing within
the first 20 minutes.

No shit! Wooww. So it's true?

Yep. Four children, he said. Also, "Singapore
Street" is a sex song.

Good grief! I want all the deets later. Quick
question. Rai always forgets the visual notes.
What's he wearing?

Blue jeans, high-shine black leather shoes, white cotton tee, suit jacket. A watch that probably costs more than my car. He had on shades, but she made him take them off.

Bwahahahaha

Oh and he's got a close-trimmed little beard thing happening. It's hot.

Focus, Micah

Sorry. Anyway, he's opening up to her. She's got some serious strategies.

Yep

No idea where this will go next, though. Lots of detours.

Buckle up, baby!

I hear that.

12

SOPHISTICATED LADY

GENE COLTRANE INTERVIEW, OCTOBER
21, 2019

The Bellweather Hotel, Studio City, CA
Audio Recording Part 3

"You're not going to like this next question."

"Way to set it up, girl! I'm on the edge of my seat."

"April 2015."

"Shit. OK, go ahead."

"You're busted for possession. Pills and cocaine. Tox screen is all sorts of indicative. Your reps say it was a moment of weakness; insiders say it was a habit. Who's right?"

"What are you asking?"

"Do you still use? Have you been using for a long time?"

"I drink. I smoke."

"And?"

(*Silence.*)

"Are you clean, Jack?"

"Right now? Yes."

"Stop dodging the question."

(*Exasperated.*) "What do you think, Munie?"

"I think we'll come back to this later."

"No—screw that. You asked the question, and you obviously want to know the answer."

"OK go for it."

"Yes, I used in 2015. No, it wasn't a—what the hell did they say—"

"A moment of weakness."

"Right. It wasn't that. I smoked my first joint when I was eighteen. By the time Lark and I were living together, I was doing coke once in a while. His deal was more serious, but there it is."

"Did you ever try to quit?"

"Twice. Once when Lark died—it scared the living shit out of me. Lasted about a year. I fell down as soon as I went back on tour."

"And the second?"

After the thing in 2015."

"Makes sense. How long did that last?"

"Maybe six months?"

(She's quiet, then pulls in a slow breath.) "That's when your father died."

"Yeah." *(A long beat of silence, then he speaks in a strained voice.)* "Can it be your turn now?"

"Absolutely. Go for it."

(The sound of water pouring and someone taking a long drink.) "The ink on the inside of your forearm—what's it mean?"

"Oh you noticed that?"

(Flirtatiously.) "It's on your body, isn't it?"

(She laughs wryly. A chair creaks, then another.) "It's the word 'Rai' in Sanskrit. I got it a couple of years ago. It means 'ray' or 'beam.' It could also mean 'queen.'"

"Wow." *(A pause.)* "So you are a ray of sunshine after all... my queen."

"I guess I am. Next question—"

"Dude, that was thirty seconds!"

"Ask me a harder one next time, then."

"You know it."

"Don't worry—I'll go in easy."

(Flirtatiously.) "I always do."

"Knock it off, Jack. Want a refill?"

"Nah. Thanks though."

(The sound of pouring, clinking, and sipping. She sighs contentedly.)

"Black, huh?"

"Yep. I stopped with the cream and sugar years ago. Now that flavor is too much."

"Why? What's it taste like?"

"It tastes like dessert."

(His voice pitches lower.) "I'll bet it does."

"What's your coffee mashup of choice?"

"Grande iced mocha with two extra shots."

"So, you're sweet?"

"Absolutely."

(Another sip.) "So tell me about *your* tattoos."

"Oh! Yeah, sure." (*A chair creaking and the ruffling of clothing.)* "Ethan, can you take this, please? I'm cool with just the tee shirt from here on out. Thanks, man." *(He laughs.)* "No jacket required, right?"

(Her voice is quiet.) "Right."

(A chair creaks again.) "Forearm first—the mermaid is for the first song I ever sold—"

"'Siren,' for P.O., right?"

(Impressed.) "Yeah! Right on. Come closer. The conga drums are for my dad. And the sphinx ... that's kind of to remind me to be calm and keep looking straight ahead."

"I like that."

"OK, upper arm." *(Another creak; she clears her throat.)* "Elouisa is my mom's name. And there's the Bahamian flag..."

"How many tats do you have?"

"Almost done. Other bicep." *(More creaking.)* "How do you like this one?"

"Whoa! Is that Duke Ellington?"

"Yep! That one's the newest. 'Sophisticated Lady' is one of my favorite pieces to play on piano."

"It's beautiful. And why the parrot beside it?"

(He laughs and groans.) "Parrot was my nickname growing up."

"Parrot? Why is that?"

"Because I mimicked everybody. I mean, like, everybody. Drove my mom crazy."

(*She giggles.*) "That's actually really cute. So any more, or have we gone through the whole library?"

"One more. Or two, if you want to see the one on my ass." (*She sighs in annoyance.*) "Kidding. Last one. Hopefully I won't stretch out this shirt too bad. At least it's a vee neck. Gotta get to my pec." (*He grunts slightly; more creaking.*) "Here. Literally a musician at heart, I guess."

(*Several beats of silence. Her voice is thick.*) "What's the song?"

"Something I wrote for my mom as a little kid."

"You never cease to surprise me, Jack." (More *silence, her sigh, then the sound of hands drumming the armrests of a chair.*) "But, unfortunately, Kindergarten Question Hour is now over. Back to the drugs."

"Fuck. Why?"

"Because it's part of your story. As you can imagine, substance abuse is a pretty frequent theme for the folks I talk to in this business."

"Shocker. OK fine, go for it."

"What I've heard a lot is that using is like a seesaw—sometimes it tips into destructiveness, or it tips the other way into sobriety, or close to it. Does that resonate at all?"

(*A pause.*) "Yeah, yeah, I get it. For a while I was like that—more early on, maybe. I'd tip too far on tour, and tip back the other way in between. But the thing is, there's no balance part. It's always moving. The only way to balance is to get off the damn thing."

"Which side are you on now? Again, we won't share this if you don't want to."

(*He heaves a long sigh.*) "After my dad died, I was on the heavy end for a while." (*His voice warms.*) "You know how when you're the heavy end of a real seesaw, your butt keeps bumping on the ground? That was me for basically all of 2016 and some of 2017 too."

"And now?"

"Now I got a little more air."

"What balances you? When you're riding the seesaw, I mean?"

(*A pause.*) "Friends. Mom. Nick Boone. Man, I don't know why that dude still hangs around with me. I've been a total shit. He's smacked my ass back into shape more than once."

"Nick's gold."

"He is."

"What else?"

(*His tone is effusive.*) "My kids. Munie, I had no idea, but being a dad is intense in the best way."

"Oh yeah?"

"Absolutely. You got kids?"

"No—never wanted them."

"Ah."

"What is it that makes you smile like that? Tell me more."

"Shit... it's just... all of it. You see this ball of energy coming at you, looking kinda like you, with all these ideas and reactions and emotions, and it's just... it's life! Right there is life."

"What's the age range, if you don't mind my asking?"

"Totally cool. Just don't publish any of their info, OK?"

"Promise."

"Thanks. Zenith is ten—he's the oldest. Lives in Missouri. The youngest is Amalia. She's four going on forty." (*He laughs.*) "I got to know Zenith first, about three years ago, and the others over time as... well... I guess as the news popped in!" (*He laughs wryly.*) "It's a boy! It's a girl! It's another boy!"

"Not your usual fatherhood experience, eh?"

"Not so much." (*Water pouring.*)

"How often do you see them?"

"Not enough—maybe every few months—but I'm starting to plan longer residencies and tours around where they all live. Two are in the States, one is in Europe, and Amalia is in Australia—"

"Wow!" (*A pause.*) "Sorry. I shouldn't be reacting."

"Nah, I get it." (*He laughs.*) "I'm saying the same thing to myself! Imagine walking up to your own kid and having her give you shit in an Australian accent."

"Ha! Sounds a little... unique."

"Good word for it. But yeah, they've shifted my priorities a lot. Seriously, it's incredible. I get this gift, and I don't want to mess it up. I've already missed a hell of a lot, you know? And even if it's hard and awkward sometimes, it's one hundred percent worth it. I want to be there... not just on paper, but really be there. Really be a father." *(He laughs airily.)* "Sorry—didn't mean to get all drippy on you."

"No, not at all. That's amazing, Jack."

"Thanks. I'm trying." *(A pause.)* "Your turn, Munie."

"All right, Jack. Hit me."

"What were you like as a kid? Were you badgering the other first graders on the playground for their deepest, darkest secrets?"

(She snort-laughs.) "Hardly. I was shy as hell."

"No way!"

"Truth. I even worked in the town library in high school. And I liked it."

"See that's a beautiful thing. Look at us. When I was sixteen I was playing jazz at midnight on school nights in clubs full of tourists, and you were shelving books in the history section. That's a good combination."

(The clink of ice in a glass; the sound of drinking.) "I don't think I could have done what you did—I'm too internal."

(Suggestively.) "I can be internal sometimes."

"Stop it."

"What?"

"That. You're flirting."

(A chair creaks; the sound of ice moving in a glass and her surprised inhale.) "What are you doing with my water, Jack?"

(He speaks in a low, intimate voice.) "Woman, I don't flirt. I seduce. And I don't try to hide it when I do." *(The sound of someone taking a long drink.)* "Ahh. Thanks." *(More ice clinking, then several beats of silence. His voice is still low.)* "You smell nice."

(She clears her throat.) "So do you. Farella? Smells sort of like that but not completely."

(Playfully.) "You been thinking about that, huh?"

(She sounds flustered.) "Jack, seriously."

"You're right. It's Farella, but with cocoa butter under it. When I get out of the shower, I rub cocoa butter in my hair and all over my skin. Everywhere. And can I tell you a secret?"

(Her voice carries a note of annoyance.) "What?"

"Come closer." *(She sighs impatiently; a chair creaks.)*

(He whispers.) "It's edible. You can lick it right off."

(She whispers back.) "I'm allergic." *(A pause, then the sound of both of them bursting into laughter.)*

Songs on this Track

Sophisticated Lady: Songwriter Duke Ellington; performed by Duke Ellington

13

——————

HEARTBEAT

GENE COLTRANE INTERVIEW, OCTOBER
21, 2019

The Bellweather Hotel, Studio City, CA
Audio Recording Part 4

"I WANT TO READ YOU A QUOTE."

"OK."

"Lots of profanity, but it's verbatim, so forgive me."

(*He chortles.*) "Come on now, girl, look who you're talking to."

"Fair enough. Here goes: 'I was nervous about working with him, no shit. He's like a fucking Mozart with songs, and I'm just some dude from Cleveland with a high school diploma who can rap a little. I thought I'd get in that session and just be all dumbed-out by Coltrane, but it was the opposite. When we got outta the studio, there was this song that came from a place deeper than I even knew I had. The brother's a musical Sigmund fucking Freud.'"

(*He laughs heartily.*) "That's gotta be Donnie Prince. Nobody else I know cusses like that."

"Ten points to Gene Coltrane—you're absolutely right. But which song?"

(*He responds quickly.*) "Heartbeat."

"Precisely."

"I remember that day real well. We were working on the lyric, and we hit on this image, and all of a sudden, the brother started to cry. The fuckin' song just wrote itself from there."

"Here's another for you. See if you can guess who this is."

(*Hands rubbing together.*) "All right. Bring it on."

"'It's like he could read me. My face, my body—sometimes even my mind. He picked up on what I wanted almost like he was clairvoyant. And then it was magic—riffing back and forth, laughing, trying different approaches to a line. He was ceaseless too. He kept going and going, digging in, tweaking one little thing after another—smoking all the time too. He didn't give up until the song sounded perfect and I was perfect inside it. He's a brilliant partner.'"

(*His tone is humble.*) "Wow. Who was that?"

"Tiyani Keith, talking about writing 'Take the Moon.'"

"Damn."

"Yeah."

(*He exhales as if smiling; his voice is warm.*) "Before we found the tune for that song, we spent a lot of time just playing around—warming up, you know?" (*He laughs warmly.*) "At one point, I started playing 'Think'—"

"Aretha Franklin?"

"Yeah, yeah. And she takes off singing, just sitting there on the couch. I swear when she got into it and started blasting, the damn windows shook."

"Wow—I'd love to have heard that."

"It was unreal." (*Silence. His voice is softer.*) "And I also remember right when we found the tune for 'Take the Moon.' She was standing in front of the piano, and I was playing and humming—just messing around. Some of the riffs didn't land—her body language didn't change. But then I tried that melody from what's now the main hook of the song. Right away, her shoulders went down, softer-like, her head tilted to the side a little, and her mouth relaxed. I saw her go from closed to open, and I knew we were on it."

"You have a gift for reading people."

"Maybe."

"Not maybe. This is proof—from those exact people. How do you do it? Is it a muscle you've developed, or more of an instinct?"

"I don't know—both?" (*A pause.*) "It's a lot like making love."

"Huh?"

"Yeah—exactly like it. When you first do it, maybe you're all preoccupied with the thing you're doing, how to do it, whatever, so you're not tuned in. Then after you get some experience and have the mechanics down better, you realize that really good sex is about listening. You've got to find the groove that she needs—find the beat she wants to dance to. That's it. Same with songwriting. If you listen, you find the right groove. Then you can make a good fucking song." (*He laughs.*) "Or a good *fucking* song."

"Hilarious."

"I know." (*Silence.*)

"That's actually a good segway into a related subject."

"Oh shit." (*They both chuckle.*) "What's that?"

"Women."

(*Playfully.*) "Ah! One of my favorite topics."

"I'm aware." (*A pause.*) "We talked earlier about how relationships have influenced and inspired your music. However, the two examples we covered spoke more to the casual side of things. Is that fair to say?"

"Yeah."

"OK. In that case, where does your deeper work come from? Are those songs also based on personal experience?"

"How do you mean?"

"Let's go back to 'Take the Moon,' for example. You and Tiyani co-wrote the music, but you put down the full lyric, correct?"

"Correct. And she did a fucking incredible job singing it."

"She did." (*A pause.*) "Jack, that's a very deep, emotional piece. It's hard for me to imagine that lyrics like '*Take the world / take the moon, take everything I am / just please stay*' come from anywhere but personal experience. Am I right?"

(*Silence.*)

"Jack?"

(*More silence.*)

"So you're happy to go into elaborate detail about the makings of a song about great sex with a random woman you met at a bar, but you clam up when it comes to an actual love song?"

(He sighs and speaks softly.) "You go first."

(She sounds exasperated.) "Fine. Go ahead."

(His voice is still soft and now colored with emotion.) "Was your hair always that color?"

"Why on earth would you ask that question?"

(A pause.) "Call it a different kind of icebreaker."

(She heaves an impatient sigh.) "When I was younger it was dark brown. I started to color it when I was about thirty-five, when it started to turn gray in places. I went through a whole lot of shades and styles for a while, and then when I was forty-two or forty-three, I stopped dying it. Now it is what it is."

(Softly.) "It's beautiful." *(Silence, then a chair creaking.)* "May I?"

(Quietly, uncertain.) "Um, OK."

(A pause.) "It's like a prism—brown, silver—right here's some red where it hits the sun from that window." *(Another pause; more creaking.)* "It has a lot to say."

(Prolonged silence.)

(He sighs.) "My turn. I wrote 'Take the Moon' for a woman I met when I was young, not long after I moved here. She showed up in my life one day, and I fell in love with her, but she couldn't bring herself to see me again. She walked away."

"Her loss."

"That's it." *(A pause.)* "Munie?"

"Yes?"

(His tone is quiet but passionate.) "I would have loved her hard." *(A long silence, followed by the sound of sniffling.)* "You OK? Here."

"Thanks." *(A nose being blown discreetly.)* "Wow, I never get emotional like this during interviews."

(Very quietly.) "Maybe it resonates with you too."

(More sniffling.) "Maybe. It's touching, Jack. Really touching."

"It's true."

"I can tell. Maybe that's why it got to me. I can feel it. Everyone should be loved like that."

"Have you been loved like that?"

(*A pause.*) "Not relevant."

"Bullshit. It's your turn, Munie. Come on."

(*A silence, then the sound of coffee pouring. She sighs long.*) "I had a fiancé once—Michael. He said he loved me like that, but he really didn't." (*A pause.*) "He loved the idea of me."

"What's that mean?"

"I suppose I... I fit nicely into his life. We had the same friends, similar interests, our parents were cut from the same cloth. It was kind of like ..."

(*A chair creaks. His voice is intimate.*) "Like what?"

"Like he'd made this Cinderella shoe out of all the things his wife should be ... and that shoe happened to fit me."

"But?"

"But I didn't like the way it felt. So eventually I broke off the engagement."

"So the answer to my question is no?"

"What?"

"I asked you if you've ever been loved like I loved that girl back then. Sounds like the answer is no."

(*She sighs, her voice pensive.*) "I guess not. I mean, it's not like I've made much time for that kind of thing, either." (*A long pause.*) "There was this one guy I kept running into. Different places, different times, and every interaction was intense."

"What happened?"

"Let's just say I didn't make the same impression on him."

"Then he's a moron."

(*She barks out a laugh.*) "Somehow I think he would have been a tough fit anyway." (*A pause and a rueful huff.*) "Next time I dive in to love I'll make sure I find the right shoes for me."

"Munie?"

(*Her voice is soft.*) "Yes?"

(*He whispers.*) "Just go fucking barefoot."

(A heavy silence falls; then the sharp intake of breath. A chair creaks. He sighs. She clears her throat.)

(His voice is light.) "I have a feeling it's going to be my turn for a while."

"Indubitably."

"Whatever the hell that means."

"It means you're absolutely right."

(He chuckles.)

"Between 2000 and 2001 you worked on a rock album with the Merry Griswolds. You co-wrote most of the songs, played multiple instruments on almost every track, provided backing vocals, and co-produced the whole thing."

"You make it sound pretty damned impressive."

"It was. At the end of 2001, they asked you to join the band, but you said no. Why?"

"I just didn't feel it."

"But then in 2002 they exploded. You could have been part of that huge global phenomenon, which was based not in small part by your work. Do you regret saying no?"

"Nah."

"Why not?"

"I go with my gut. One hundred percent of the time. And it's never wrong. If I'd joined the Griswolds, I'd have done those two albums, toured everywhere, and made a shit-ton more money than I did on my own at that point, but it wouldn't have been me. Plus, I would have missed out on some even bigger opportunities."

"Such as?"

"Meeting that girl I just told you about."

"But she's the one who got away."

(A long pause, his voice low.) "Is she?"

Songs **on this Track**

Think: Songwriters Aretha Franklin and Ted White; performed by Aretha Franklin

14

BREAK #4

Giiiiirrrrrlll!

What?

I have no idea what in the actual hell is going on right now.

What do you mean?

Well first off, they've been using each other's personal names this whole time. He's calling her Munie, like Glenys does, and she's calling him Jack.

Huh?

Yeah, since the first segment. And now—I'm telling you straight up—he is flirting with her HARD.

No shit

Seriously. I wish I could see into that room.

Is she OK?

Yeah—I just talked to her at the last break. She looks fine, but sometimes she sounds kind of… flustered. Like he's getting under her skin for real. AND she got teary just a little minute ago.

Rai? She's the ice woman.

I know it.

This is either going to turn out to be an award-winning interview or an epic clusterfuck.

Mmm hmmm.

15

___

POR ENCONTRAR UN BESO TUYO

GENE COLTRANE INTERVIEW, OCTOBER 21, 2019

The Bellweather Hotel, Studio City, CA
Audio Recording Part 5

"Worst interview ever."

"Oh come on!"

(*His voice is playful.*) "What? I have just spilled so much shit to you, Munie. It's the least you could do. Throw a dog a bone, girl. I won't say a word. In fact... hold up. Do you need someone to be in here for the recording?"

"No—it's just audio going right into this laptop. I've got it."

"Cool." (*Loudly.*) "Hey Ethan, could we have the suite, maybe?" (*More softly.*) "That OK with you?"

(*She sounds slightly confused.*) "Um, sure. Micah—feel free to head out. Thanks."

(*They're quiet until the doors close with a click.*)

"All right, you may dish openly. You want to turn off the recording first? So it's not 'on the record?'"

"Good idea. I'll turn off the laptop but keep the phone backup going. That one's just for me." (*The sound of rustling and keys clicking, then a laptop cover closing.*) "OK, you can take off your mike now. Just stay close to that little one attached to the phone here on the table, OK?"

"Got it." *(More rustling, then the sound of two lapel mikes being placed on a table. A long, heavy silence.)*

(His voice is quiet, his tone low and intimate.) "Let's go." *(More silence. His voice lightens.)* "Worst interview. Just don't say it's me."

(She chuckles.) "It's not … yet." *(A long pause; she sighs.)* "David Regent Barnes. Man, that must be at least twelve or thirteen years ago now."

"Don't know him."

"He hasn't done much in a while, but back then he was in a pretty popular BBC series. He was also a first-class douche bag."

"What happened?"

"I was just about a year and a half into the journalism business—I was doing general entertainment then—and they sent me to talk to him about the new season of his show." *(A pause.)* "We always do research before an interview, right? For example, I spent about three weeks getting ready for today—"

"I can tell."

"So when I looked into his past work, I noticed he'd done a lot of commercials before his big break." *(Silence.)*

(His voice is soothing.) "It's all good, Munie. Keep going."

(She lets out a long, deep breath.) "I asked him about it—some conceptual question about the change in his professional approach from then to now." *(An audible swallow.)* "And right there in a room full of cameramen and sound techs, his handlers and my colleagues, he tells me that it's the most sophomoric, idiotic question he's ever heard, and how dare I resort to something so basic and disrespectful."

"No fucking way."

"Yeah. Then he told my manager, who was right there, to step in and finish the interview."

"Oh shit. What an asshole. I'm sorry Munie."

"Yeah. I mean, two weeks later he got caught with a prostitute in the bathroom of an art gallery in Sweden, so I guess what goes around comes around."

"Oh no—THAT guy??"

"Yes!"

"Oh shit! That was an epic story. The dude's a total fucknut."

"Well yeah, I know that now, but back then it almost made me quit journalism."

"Are you serious?"

"Yeah. He really got to me." *(Silence.)*

"One dick made you doubt yourself that much?"

(She blows out a breath.) "Well, it wasn't long after I'd had another horrible boss—in my old job, pre-journalism. She made me feel like I was worthless every single day."

"Why'd you let her?"

"What do you mean?"

"That wasn't her call. Or David Regent Fucknut's. Or anyone's." *(A chair creaks.)* "Munie—you gotta know how amazing you are. Do you?" *(Another creak; his voice lower.)* "Do you?"

(She responds slowly.) "Maybe more now, but not as much then." *(She pauses, then chuckles airily.)* "I'm just glad I never quit."

(Warmly.) "Me too." *(More creaking, then the sound of hands drumming against thighs.)* "My turn."

"Thanks." *(She heaves a heavy sigh; the sound of pouring, sipping, and clinking.)* "I'd love to go back to that period of 2015 when you were clean."

"OK cool."

"Am I right that, even though it didn't get released until the end of last year because of the label acquisition, you wrote and produced the entire *Blue Sky* album inside those six months or so?"

"Absolutely."

"Excuse my directness, but how in the hell did you do that?"

(He laughs.) "I was deep in the zone, man. When I left rehab, I basically hung out at home and at the studio just to stay away from temptation. That's the truth of it. And the songs just came."

"Why the change, though? You made a huge pivot from R&B back to straight-up jazz. It surprised everyone."

(He's silent for a few beats.) "A couple of interviewers have asked me

that, and I've told them it was basically just that I burned out on R&B. But that's not really it."

"OK."

(Silence; he speaks slowly, carefully.) "When I'm using, everything is at this basic level. It's like that picture of an iceberg where you only see the top part, you know? But when I'm clean, the rest of the whole damned thing shows up. It's hard, because it's like the *Titanic* with all the shit that comes with it, but musically it's... incredible. What comes through is totally clear, and really fucking deep. It's almost like I can't write fast enough." *(A pause.)* "Does that make sense?"

"I think so. Like drugs are a filter, and when you're sober, the filter's gone?"

"Yeah—exactly. But it's even more than that. I get these little amazing gifts—notes, beats, progressions, images I wouldn't have found otherwise and didn't know I needed, but that change the whole course of the song."

"For example?"

(Silence. He blows out a long breath. More silence. His voice takes on a gentle, sober tone.) "Like that little gold fleck in your eyes. If I'd never seen it, I wouldn't know I needed to keep seeing it. But now I do." *(A heavy quiet falls. He speaks softly.)* "Your turn, Munie."

(A chair creaks. The sound of heels retreating. Her voice comes from a distance.) "Those chairs are awful. My back is killing me."

"They're loud, too."

"Yeah." *(She sighs long and vocalizes, as if stretching. He lets out a low groan.)*

"OK, Jack. Go for it."

"What are your three must-have qualities in a man?"

(Incredulous.) "Isn't that a little personal?"

"So is asking about my drug history."

"Touché."

"What?"

"Touché. It's French. It kind of means 'you got me.'"

"Cool. You speak French?"

"No, just Portuguese and a little Italian."

"Portuguese?"

"My dad's from Brazil. 'Raimunda' is a Brazilian name. 'Hai-MOON-duh.'"

(A chair creaks. His footsteps retreat. His voice now comes from further away as well.) "That's really hot, 'Hai-moon-duh.'"

(Her tone is shaky, tentative.) "Very good."

(Seductively.) "I caught a little Spanish growing up—especially being in my family's band. The ladies in the audience loved it."

"Oh yeah?"

(A pause.) "Yeah. Give me your hand."

"What are you doing, Jack?"

"Demonstrating. You speak Spanish along with that Portuguese?"

"Some."

"Good. We used to sing 'Bésame Mucho' a lot back in the day, but then my cousin made a song out of this old Spanish poem he found. We did it a capella. Like this." *(He begins to sing slowly and with surprising elegance.)*

"Por encontrar un beso tuyo, / ¿qué daría yo? / ¡Un beso errante de tu boca / muerta para el amor."

(He speaks in a whisper, barely audible.) "What would I give for a kiss that came from your lips."

"Jack..."

"I'm not done. There's another verse."

(He sings again.) *"Y por besar tus muslos castos, / ¿qué daría yo? / Cristal de rosa primitiva, / sedimento de sol.)"*

(He speaks again, his voice even more intimate.) "And what would I give to kiss your beautiful thighs, that pure rose crystal, a particle of the sun." *(He chuckles in a low voice.)* "Or something like that."

(Heavy silence, then movement, impossible to make out. More silence.)

(She whispers.) "Please stop."

(A silent beat.) "OK."

(The subtle sound of a slow kiss being placed somewhere, then her quick intake of breath. Her footsteps start back to the mike, more rapidly this time; his follow a few beats behind. Two chairs creak. Heavy silence follows for several seconds.)

(Her tone is detached and professional.) "Why do you have to be so charming?"

"It's a curse." *(He laughs once, then becomes quiet.)*

"That's not a joke, Jack. The smiling, the flirting, the seducing—it's like you're always doing a show for someone, like you don't think just being you is enough of a draw." *(She lets out a dry, airy huff.)* "Like just talking to me wasn't enough. You had to take it up a notch and do what you just did. Why?"

"Shit, Munie, come on."

"No. I want to go there."

"I just did it!"

"But why?"

"Hell, I don't know!"

"Bullshit. Why, Jack?"

(He blurts out in frustration.) "I'm a performer! What do you want?"

"So over there by the window just now—that was a performance for my benefit?" *(A pause. Her voice gets slightly louder.)* "Were they all just performances, Jack?"

"No!"

"Then what? We can't just talk? You don't think simply talking to you impresses me?"

(His tone becomes dim.) "What if it doesn't?"

"OK ... what if it doesn't? Does that make you less?"

(He's silent.)

"Let me ask you a question you may never have thought of before."

"That'll be the 57th one today."

"Who loves *you*?"

(Silence.)

"All these women you've fallen for, slept with, some of whom are now the mothers of your children? Jen Marini? The adoring fans who scream when you smile and sing and move your hips? Do they really love you?"

(More silence.)

"Come on, Jack. Think. Who are the people who truly love the real you?"

(He's quiet for a long beat.) "My mom. My sisters. My brother."

"Keep going."

(A pause; he sighs.) "The guys in the band. The crew I hung out with growing up." *(He lets out a small chuckle.)* "Uncle Esai. Nick." *(There's a note of vulnerability in his voice.)* "Yeah."

(She speaks gently.) "And do you have to put on a show for any of them?"

(A sniffle.) "No."

"And I don't need one either. Hear that, Jack. Please." *(She whispers.)* "You're so very much without it."

(Silence. Emotion colors his voice.) "Give me your hand again." *(A pause.)* "Please."

(Her tone is uncertain.) "OK."

(The sound of a chaste kiss being placed.) "Thank you. I hear that." *(A pause; he takes a long, shaky breath.)* "Now can we please fucking talk about something light, like whether I like puppies or kittens or some shit?"

"I'll do you one better—it's time for lunch."

"Now you're talking, girl!"

(Noise around the microphone, then the recording clicks off.)

Songs on this Track

Bésame Mucho: Lyrics and music by Consuelo Velázquez; performed by Javier Solis

Poems on this Track

Untitled [Por encontrar un beso tuyo], Federico García Lorca

SESSION #5

They just kicked us out.

Excuse me?

Gene and Rai told us to leave.

Why? Did you guys interrupt or something?

Not at all. Gene asked something about her personal life, she got shy I guess, then they asked us to leave so they could talk privately.

What the hell? Do you think she's all right in there by herself?

She wouldn't have told me to leave if not. But honey—I'm still sitting right outside this door in the hallway in case she needs me.

I love you.

I know.

17

———

QUINTESSENCE

GENE COLTRANE INTERVIEW, OCTOBER 21, 2019

The Bellweather Hotel, Studio City, CA
Audio Recording Part 6

"Is it on?" *(Distortion, sounds of movement and rustling.)*

"Yeah, I think so. I'll keep it right in the middle here. Just try not to spill anything on it, OK? I just bought this phone."

(He chuckles.) "No promises."

(She chuckles in response. The sound of heels against tile. She sighs contentedly.) "Oh wow. *Theta* really knows how to do it up right. This is beautiful. And we have the whole balcony to ourselves?"

"Yeah. No need to go inside the actual restaurant, either. Ethan said to go back to the interview room the same way we came. Right down the breezeway."

"The usual game of 'hide the celebrity,' eh?"

"Exactly. Please." *(The sound of chair legs scraping against the floor, then rustling.)*

"Thanks." *(His footsteps, then another scrape of chair legs and more rustling.)*

"Don't you ever get tired of that?"

"What?"

"Having to duck around in the shadows, always on guard in case the paparazzi pop out of a shrubbery somewhere?"

(He laughs airily.) "Yeah, sometimes. But—and I don't mean this to sound all trippy and egotistical—I've lived like this for over a decade, so it's kind of old hat. And most of my friends are in all these 'hidden places' now, anyway." *(Playfully.)* "Although sometimes I do sneak out for good food!"

"Yeah? Like what?"

"There's this tiny little pizza joint in New York City—Nick Boone told me about it. It's in—"

"Hell's Kitchen. No sign, yellow aluminum awning, right?"

(Surprised.) "You know it??!"

(A pause. Her voice is dimmer than before and slightly sad.) "Nick told me about it too. That place is amazing. Good call, Jack. You really are a foodie."

"Absolutely." *(A silent beat.)* "What's wrong?"

(More silence; she clears her throat.) "Nothing. Just hungry, I think."

"Let's get some food, then. What are you looking at?"

"Now? Pizza, damn you."

(He laughs loudly.) "Same here. But it is what it is today, and I'll need my energy if you're going to rip me a new one in round two this afternoon."

"I'll go easy. Maybe. And I'm going with the seared salmon salad."

(He sighs.) "You know, no matter how much money I make, I'll never be OK spending thirty-five dollars on a piece of fish."

(She laughs.) "Especially since you probably grew up eating the morning's catch!"

"Exactly!" *(He laughs. The sound of footsteps.)* "Wine?"

"Love to, but never when I'm interviewing like this. I need all my wits about me. Club soda with lime is about as crazy as I get."

"Maybe I should skip it too, so that you don't make me spill stuff I don't want to."

"Too late."

(He laughs again.) "Touché." *(She giggles.)* "May I?"

"Sure."

"The salmon salad and a club soda with lime for the beautiful lady, and I'll do the miso cod with a glass of chenin blanc. Thanks, man."

(*A new person's voice.*) "Very good, sir." (*Footsteps retreat.*)

"Chenin blanc, huh? Pretty highbrow."

"I have Heineken in the fridge at home."

(*She laughs deep and loud.*)

"Damn, I love your laugh." (*Awkward silence.*) "So, what the fuck do we talk about when we're just real people?"

"Well, we've established that you're a foodie and a wine snob—"

"Hey!"

"Am I lying?"

"No. But you should taste my mojito."

(*Saucily.*) "Is that a come-on?"

(*A silent beat.*) "Oh snap!" (*He erupts into a high-pitched cackle.*) "Shit ..."

"Sorry—you just laid that one out there. Made it too easy. Let's see..." (*Fingers drumming on the table.*) "What's the most beautiful thing that comes to mind when you think about home?"

"Bahamas?"

"Yeah."

"Graffiti."

"What?"

"Yeah, totally."

(*Her voice is low, relaxed.*) "Tell me."

"Back home, we have tons of street artists, and they try and outdo each other by painting murals on the sides of the old buildings around town. But this isn't your average New York City subway shit. It's like fine art—all these hues and details. It even changes when the light hits it at different angles. Like the images are so real you could touch them, or walk right into the scene. I have no idea how they do it, but it's beautiful."

"I can just picture it."

"I'd love to show you."

(A lengthy silence; the sound of footsteps, then the sound of glasses placed on the tabletop.)

"To beauty."

(His tone is low.) "Yeah, Munie, to beauty." *(Glasses clinking together, then a long, quiet beat.)* "I've talked a lot today."

"And the day is young."

"Right." *(The sound of a utensil on a plate.)* "So let me listen for a while. Let's talk about you."

"Fair enough, OK. I have to admit that I don't really like talking about myself, though."

(His tone is low, intimate.) "Why not? I'll listen all day."

"Jack ..."

"Fine." *(A pause.)* "I want to hear about that horrible boss."

"Why?"

"Because it matters to you."

"Geez, Jack."

"Come on, woman. You grilled me harder than that all morning."

"Fine." *(She sighs; the sound of silverware clinking onto a plate.)* "She was a couple of years younger than me, right out of business school. I had a few more years of experience, but she had more clout. I don't know if she didn't like me, or was threatened by me, or what, but every day, she found a way to belittle or gaslight me. And I took it all in. I'm just thankful it was only for about ten months—after that, I got a job in journalism, so I could escape."

"Why do you keep escaping?"

"What do you mean?"

"This bitch, John Regent Fucknut—they both made you want to run. Why not just stare them down? They ain't nothing."

(A pause.) "I don't know. I've always been kind of a perfectionist, I guess. I was an only child, and my folks were both big brains—a scientist and a psychologist—"

"Damn!"

"Yeah. And so there was always kind of this tacit expectation that I'd be great at everything. So when I'm not ... still as an adult sometimes it's easy to feel like a failure if I'm not perfect. I guess it makes me run from situations where I'm not totally in the driver's seat." *(Silence.)* "So there you go."

(He laughs.) "Fucking childhood, right?"

(She chuckles lightly.) "Right. But didn't you get any of that, growing up with performers?"

(A pause; he sighs.) "In a different way. It was less 'perfect' and more 'worthwhile.' My dad's expression was always, 'If you ain't the best, you ain't nothing.'"

"Jack, that's horrible." *(She's silent for several seconds, then she begins again, more quietly.)* "Is that what's behind that insane work ethic of yours?" *(Silence.)* "It is, isn't it? You feel like if what you produce isn't over the top, it's not worth anything? Like *you* don't have worth if you're not at a ten all the time?"

(More silence; her tone soothing.) "He didn't leave because you're not enough. That's not true."

(His voice is pained.) "That's a hard one to swallow when you're a fifteen year-old kid." *(Silence.)* "Please change the subject, Munie."

(Her voice is still gentle.) "Of course. Ask me something."

(A pause. He clears his throat.) "I love this song. Will you dance with me, Munie Paley?"

"Jack..."

"Come on, no ulterior motive, just to lighten things up a little. Just until the expensive fish comes."

(She laughs quietly.)

(His tone is vulnerable.) "Please? I could use the break."

(She sighs long in resignation.) "OK, but just until we get our food."

"Deal." *(Chair legs scraping, his footsteps.)* "May I?"

"Thanks." *(More chair scraping, then heeled and non-heeled footsteps retreating. Their voices come from a small distance away.)*

"This OK? We can hear better under the speaker."

"Yeah." *(A few quiet beats.)* "I don't think I've ever heard this song."

"Ah! This is some early Quincy."

"Really? I love it. What's it called?"

(A pause; he whispers.) "It's 'Quintessence.'"

(She whispers back.) "Wow."

"Yeah."

(Several moments of silence, punctuated by soft footsteps.)

"You still haven't answered my last question, you know."

"What's that?"

"Three qualities in a man. You can use your man as an example if you want."

"I don't have one." *(A long silent beat.)* "But any man of mine needs to have… a genuine heart… a sense of humor… and kindness."

"Doesn't sound like a tough enough laundry list."

"Meaning?"

"You're going too easy. You deserve more than 'nice and funny.'"

"Those aren't good qualities?"

"Of course they are, but for fuck's sake look at you. You got it all— a huge brain, a beautiful personality, and a body to match. Even if you are a ballbuster in interviews." *(A pause.)* "You're the absolute whole equation, Raimunda Paley. Know that's true. And don't settle for any man who doesn't rate you."

(Slightly off-kilter.) "Jack…"

(His tone is low, serious.) "Munie."

(Strongly.) "OK then—what do you look for in a woman?"

"You."

"Stop it."

"I'm dead serious. I've never been more honest than this afternoon. I've never felt like I could be. This here … this is like nothing else I can remember." *(Rustling; the bottom of a shoe scraping the floor. She lets out a squeak and a giggle.)* "And it's my turn. Who do you text first in the morning?"

"If it's a weekday, my editor."

"Right. Shit. Wrong way to ask it." *(A pause.)* "Who do you text when you got a random thought you want to tell someone?"

"Glenys."

"Then who's your crew?"

"My what?"

"You know, your crew. The people you hang out with when you're not making celebrities cry."

"You haven't cried yet."

(*His voice is intimate.*) "I haven't kissed you goodbye yet." (*Silence.*) "So who, Munie?"

(*Slightly dazed.*) "Who... ?"

"Who are your people? Who calls you 'Munie' besides me and Glenys?"

"My folks moved to Colorado a long time ago, and no other family is local."

"That wasn't my question."

(*Flustered.*) "What was your question then, Jack?"

(*His voice is a heated whisper.*) "Who sees you without that suit on? Who do you get drunk with, or go bowling with? Who makes you dinner after a shitty day at work? Who gets the huge fucking honor of knowing the whole woman in there?"

(*Silence.*)

"Who holds your beautiful body at night, Munie?"

(*Whispering; her voice is unsteady.*) "Jack, please."

"Because woman, you deserve all of that, and I wish like hell I was the one to give it to you."

"Stop... this isn't..."

(*His voice is low but urgent.*) "Own it, Munie. There's something here—something big—and you know it. Do you feel that?" (*He whispers softly.*) "That?"

(*A long silence, then heeled footsteps; her voice is even further away.*) "OK then, Jack. In that case, what are you looking for in yourself? You tell me I need a man who rates me—who's the man you want to be?"

"What do you mean?"

"Is it the player who walked in here today with the expensive clothes and the shades, or is it the compelling person I'm talking to now? Is it the guy who agreed to an appearances-only girlfriend but is so lonely he sleeps around on the road, or the beautiful, romantic soul who wrote 'Take the Moon' for Tiyani Keith?"

(*Silence.*)

"Is it the addict in the tabloids or the man who paid for an entire new fucking school in his hometown, Jack? Who are you? Who do you want to be?"

"Munie, please. I can't..."

(She sighs; the sound of heels. Their voices come from the same place again.) "I'm sorry. I am. That was too far. I just..."

"You care. I get it. But understand, Munie, what you're asking is deeper than I can get to in this conversation, today, this week, this year. That's a lifetime answer. But I'll go this far—all those good guys are there. They're there." *(A pause.)* "And I'm not letting them go. I promise."

(Relieved.) "That's good. Truce?" *(Silence.)* "Well, Jack? Aren't you going to shake on it? Don't leave me hanging here."

(Sudden shuffling; her surprised inhale, followed by a long silence. Her voice is small.)

"Jack... "

(An intimate whisper.) "Munie."

(Another long silence, then movement, impossible to make out, dotted by his vocalization. After several seconds, the sound of sudden heeled footsteps.) "I can't do this."

"Why?"

"Come on, Jack. Seriously."

"Fuck the interview. It's not like I'm the biggest name you ever worked with anyway."

"It's more complicated than that."

"What then? The lifestyle? Those women?"

"No, of course not."

"Then what's stopping you?"

(Silence.)

"Maybe I'm just not worth it, Munie. The drugged-up musician on the verge of washout. Just like they're all saying. I got nothing left to give that anyone wants."

(Acerbically.) "You really do believe that, don't you?"

(Sarcastically.) "Why wouldn't I?"

(She's louder, her tone angry.) "Let me tell you why. Because you have more depth in you than any of those fools could imagine, but

you won't let it out. You're covering anything vulnerable in glitz, swagger, humor, and coke—but what you need to do is get naked, Jack. Show me, show the world, exactly who you are in there, even if it hurts." (*Heels stepping quickly toward the table; her voice is now closer to the mike.*) "Especially if it hurts. I have to go."

(*His footsteps coming toward the table; his voice closer to the mike.*) "Please don't." (*Whispering, emotional.*) "Please."

(*Silence, then the sound of a kiss being placed.*)

"Jack..."

"What if..."

"What?"

"What if it's ugly, Munie?"

(*A long quiet beat. Her voice is soft; she sounds as if she's crying.*) "It's not. And do you know how I know that?"

(*Silence.*)

"Because I know you. I know the sweet soul who dried my tears in the back room of a record store in Via Clara almost twenty years ago."

"What?"

"I know the beautiful man who wanted to understand—truly wanted to know me—the day we first made love in his bedroom in Laurel Canyon..."

"Oh no..."

"...and I know the version of you I laughed with and ate pizza with at that tiny little hole in the wall pizza joint before we made love so passionately in my hotel room."

(*He gasps.*) "Glenys!" (*A long silence; his words come out choked.*) "Oh no... no no no no. Wait... Oh Munie... oh God. It was you..." (*A pause; his voice is a reedy whisper.*) "It was always you." (*He lets out a sob.*)

"It's OK. You were on a different path then. I get it. And I'm not saying any of this to shame you, Jack. Not at all." (*A pause.*)

(*He sounds as if he's desperate.*) "Fuck. Munie, listen."

"Jack, look at me." (*He inhales raggedly.*) "I'm saying it because there's a reason I kept coming back to you, even if you didn't remember me. I knew you were good, I knew your essence was so pure. I..." *(Silence; her voice cracks.)* "I felt you in my heart, Jack. I felt you. Right here."

(He lets out a choked exhale; a long pause follows.) "Munie, listen to me, please."

"No, you don't have to explain. But now it's your turn. Show us, Jack. Show us all those beautiful things inside you. The ones I know are there. And please love yourself. You're so worth it."

(Silence, then rustling and heavy distortion. Heels clicking quickly on tile and rhythmic scratching against the microphone.)

(His voice is now far away, breaking with emotion.) "Munie... just... please stay..."

(More heels and distortion, a door closing, and her single sob. The recording clicks off.)

Songs **on this Track**

Quintessence: Songwriter Quincy Jones; performed by Quincy Jones and his Orchestra

PART III

LOVE SONG

18

A SONG FOR YOU

February 2022
Los Angeles, CA

Glenys MacKenzie was a bona fide Popcorn Hog. She had a stealth attack style, too. Every time Munie got a kernel stuck in the back of her throat (which was often), she'd guzzle a bunch of water in order to loosen it, then turn back to find a dip in the bowl roughly equivalent in size to the pile of popcorn in Glenys' hands.

"What?"

"Can't you just grab a couple of kernels at a time?"

"It's not sanitary! That's exponentially more times the hand would come into contact with the food. It's simple science."

"Then why not put yours in a separate bowl in the first place?"

"Well then we're not properly sharing, are we?"

Useless. But A. it wasn't the first time this was happening (in fact, it was a regular occurrence when Glenys visited); and B. there were better things to discuss at the moment, like who would be best and worst dressed, most and least political, and most and least "all live" during the evening's *American Music Awards* broadcast. They were 75 minutes in, and so far there were six contenders for "relatively sufferable," two "absolute asshats," and one recipient of the "stop being a celebrity and start campaigning already" award. A rocking start from all perspectives.

"I have to pee. No need to pause." That's what happens when you drink half a gallon of water in an effort to dislodge stuck popcorn. As Munie was washing her hands, the peanut gallery beckoned from the living room.

"Come see, Mun! It's the arsehole you wrote about—that Gene chap from the club."

Oh shit. Of course. It's the *American Music Awards*. The likelihood of a celebrity with the girth of Gene Coltrane being in attendance and getting at least a passing camera shot from the audience was extremely high.

She tried to keep her quavering voice steady, even as her knees started to shake. "Hold on—pause it? Be there in a sec."

She stared at her flushed face in the mirror, wondering why in the hell she hadn't already told Glenys everything. She *always* told her about everything even slightly meaningful in her life—one-night stands, mistaken identities, even dog poop on her favorite shoe—but for some reason, she'd kept the events of both that pivotal day in Studio City and the preceding history to herself.

But even if she hadn't shared it, she'd relived it ... over and over again since October 2019. Their words, their touches, his eyes, and the hole in her heart that opened the moment she left him on that balcony—the hole that still sat gaping inside her chest—it was all right there. Always right there. She could clearly see his pained, pleading face in her mind's eye, hear the crack in his voice as he begged her not to leave. She had purposely avoided reading about him or following his career over the last two and a half years in an effort to subdue the constant narrative, and it had actually started to work a little. But just a little.

She closed her eyes and took three deep breaths. Opening them again to re-assess her reflection, she found someone slightly flushed but no longer manic looking back at her. Better. OK, this was not a big deal. She could look at a passing shot of Jack in his finery, dimples firing for the cameras, and remain cool as a cucumber. Done.

She climbed back up on the sofa as serenely as possible, tucked her legs under her, and cuddled back into the seat wielding the now almost-empty popcorn bowl. Snacky reinforcement was a requirement right now, so Glenys would just have to accept it. "All righty, what'cha got?" she piped with all the nonchalance she could muster.

It was a good thing Glenys was talking as she unpaused the action, because Munie was instantly frozen in place. The screen was filled with a still image of an album cover, Jack in the center, sax around his neck, gaze off in the distance. White shirt and pants on a pale, retro blue background. Simple and elegant. The album title read *Studio City Songs,* and the words at the bottom of the screen read "Gene Coltrane, 2022 Music Evolution Award Winner." Oh no, this wasn't just a quick camera pan. Munie could barely breathe.

"Is that him? Looks like he's cleaned up a good bit—done fairly well for himself lately as well, yeah? Must've been that top-notch journalism, eh Mun?" Glenys began to laugh heartily, but stopped as soon as she realized that not one iota of her merriment had made its way to the other side of the couch. "Mun?"

Munie was transfixed, watching and listening as a member of the R&B group Lowdown narrated through a pictorial retrospective of Jack's career. The teen virtuoso sax player in the family band; the young gig musician; the emerging pop star; the seminal writer and producer—it was a kaleidoscopic view of his life, spinning in front of her to the backdrop of his own music.

"Mun, what is it?" Munie just shook her head, eyes fixed on the screen. One look at Munie's face as she watched Gene Coltrane walk onstage toward the mike told Glenys everything she needed to know. And she kept silent, giving her friend the wide berth she needed.

He was dressed just as conservatively as he had been on the album cover, this time in black pants and a suit jacket with a simple white tee shirt underneath. She took in his calm demeanor, his quietness, the lack of any of the flash and dazzle he'd worn on his sleeve the day of the interview. His clean-shaven face was noticeably fuller, healthier, his form lean and strong. With a demure smile that tore at her heart, he accepted his trophy.

She watched him watch the audience favor him with a long, loud applause, his head dipping in what looked like mild embarrassment every few seconds as the cacophony of clapping continued. Everything about him was less of an inferno than she remembered, yet still his eyes blazed. When the applause finally died down and he began his acceptance speech, it was in a voice so low and quiet—so real—that it shocked Munie's ears.

"Thank you. Wow... damn." He looked shyly at the trophy in his hands, returned his gaze to the audience, then combed the fingers of his right hand down the sides of his mouth in a gesture she now knew well.

"A few years ago, I didn't think I'd be here. At all. In fact, it was the opposite. I couldn't write a word, didn't want to play a note, but bigger than that, my whole spirit was stuck." He looked out beyond the audience for a moment, thinking.

"Sometimes redemption is a word. Sometimes it's an action, or maybe even a goal you have. My redemption was a connection. It's like... like when you slide into a groove that's completely right, just exactly the way it's supposed to be." He nodded, as if only to himself. "Yeah. Like that. For me, redemption was feeling that groove, knowing it was possible. My redemption was..." He looked down again for a long moment, as if trying to collect himself, "...it was seeing that possibility... that little fleck of gold... in someone else's eyes."

Munie went cold and hot all at once.

"And sometimes," Jack suddenly smiled a full, dimpled grin, the sight dawning across her heart like a warm morning, "sometimes redemption can have a sharp-ass tongue. But that's good too. A song gotta have a hook, right?" He paused again, a self-deprecating laugh escaping his lips.

"Look, I'm not great at talking like this, so if it's OK with you, I'd rather say it with the piano." Of course, the crowd immediately erupted into cheers, which continued as Jack walked over to a grand piano at the side of the stage, set his trophy on the floor behind it, and sat down. Adjusting the piano mike, he continued.

"Sometimes, another artist's words say it best, so I'mma borrow from two of the greats today. This mashup is for a woman whose name has been on my heart since she first gave it to me. I thought I'd lost her, but she was right there all the time. Right in front of me. I just didn't see her."

He paused, looking down, then continued. "Sometimes it takes a lifetime to get it right. I'm just thankful I get the chance now. This song is about redemption. About connection. About possibility. About when it's right. About love. This song is for the woman I love. Then. Now. Always."

She recognized the classic "A Song for You" from the first line, sung with Jack's beautifully-broken-and-put-back-together soul and a single opening chord from the piano. She knew by heart the words that were about to come to her, for her, from him in that perfect voice. And so she listened with her whole body and spirit, tears rolling down her face.

It was as if he was seeing her with his eyes closed, her image as clear to him as was her memory of his warm hand on hers. The camera panned close to Jack's face as he continued to sing, seemingly unaware of the room and everyone in it, lost in the song.

After the first chorus, his playing became a rainfall of notes, then cascaded into a kaleidoscope of complex chords and progressions, landing at last in a melody that fell with familiarity on her ear. Bringing his lips close to the microphone, he spoke two words before he began to sing: "I remember."

His next word was the title of the song she least expected him to offer, but one that fit perfectly into the hole in their past. He sang it in almost a whisper, befitting this stripped-down, austere rendition. "*Woman.*"

The lyrics were everything—a mea culpa, a confession, a plea for forgiveness—all wrapped in a message for Munie and only Munie, explaining to her in music that he now, finally, saw their time

together, felt their repeated connections in the annals of his heart—
that he had now walked the same path she had.

But that wasn't all. As the chorus crashed in, his voiced soared, his
full-chested declaration of love a shout across the auditorium and the
world. The words "I love you" were never uttered more beautifully.

Just when she found she could no longer breathe, Jack made a
smooth transition back to "A Song for You." He paused before the
final chorus, the entire auditorium silent and rapt for several seconds.
Munie couldn't move. At length, he began to sing again, softly, slowly,
tenderly; she watched a single tear roll down his cheek. He effort-
lessly floated the last note toward the heavens on a beautiful falsetto,
caressed the keys once more, and let his hands fall to his lap, head
bent. The audience was silent, then riotous with applause as the stage
went dark.

Munie turned away from the Doritos ad that flashed on the
screen and let out a sob, falling into Glenys' arms. They talked for the
next three hours with the TV off.

SONGS on This Track

A Song for You: Lyrics and music by Leon Russell; performed by
Donny Hathaway

Woman: Lyrics and music by John Lennon; performed by Ozzy
Osbourne

19

BRING IT ON HOME TO ME

June 2022
Nickles Boone's House, Hollywood Hills, CA

Munie hated this celebrity shit.

Fake smiles, fake boobs, men with dye jobs that are never subtle (if it's so black that it glows in the dark, it's clearly not your natural color), and meaningless chatter with razor-sharp undertones. It was like walking over a blanket of glass shards while balancing a martini glass in both hands—and Munie didn't normally even drink.

However, work was work, and occasionally being able to get inside the minds of rich, eccentric and (in some cases) truly talented people also meant getting inside their mansions for ridiculous Hollywood parties. *Hell, maybe a good story will come out of it*, she thought to herself as she parallel parked seamlessly into a tiny spot on a treacherous hillside curve. These driving hazards she could do without too. Risking life and limb for the LA rich and their "I need a cliff and my own ocean view" insanity was getting almost as old as ignoring neon black beard dye.

At least this party had a tribe of allies involved, however. After finishing a sixteen-month documentary on legendary music producer Nickles Boone, for which she damned well better get an Emmy nod, she'd apparently been elevated to his "permanent friends" group, and as it followed, the invitation list for his eighty-second birthday party. And regardless of how much she abhorred this kind of hob-nobbing with the upper crust, if it meant doing a solid for Nick, who now held a dear, sweet place in her heart, she was totally on board. The rest of the divas and Slick Ricks she could deal with handily—after eighteen years in the music journalism business, not much got under her skin.

Nickles was a cool cat—real and good—a man with an absolute shit-ton of life experience and the musical chops of a prodigy. He also loved women and poker, which made for some nice juice and wiggle in his narrative. Apparently that quality extended to his celebration festivity of choice as well. Munie walked through the cavernous foyer and a sitting room filled with awards and gold records to find Nickles at the dining room table, cards in his hand and side chicks at his flank, the sound system playing Sam Cooke's "Bring It On Home to Me" in the background. Nickles looked up, saw her there, and hollered with glee.

"Baby girl! Get on in here now!"

Nickles had the biggest smile you could imagine. It went literally from one ear to the other, and it was all aimed at her in that moment. Spryer than his years, he jumped up from the table to hug her and kiss her loudly on both cheeks.

"Thank you for being here. You just made my day," he crooned, hands on her arms in a gentle, grandfatherly squeeze.

"How could I miss it, Nick? After all we've been through?" She returned his affection with a gentle tug on his elbows, while Nickles, in true Nickles style, tipped his head back to laugh long and loud.

It was in that little slice of open space beside Nickles' head that the eyes came into view, staring steely-eyed straight at her.

Straight into her.

Jack.

Her mouth was suddenly a desert, her feet rooted to the floor.

Jack's gaze didn't waver one iota—it continued in a long, penetrating pulse right into the deepest part of her. It was all she could see.

There'd been no communication after the interview—not a word, not a note for two years and four months—nothing until that damned awards broadcast in February. Then nothing in the four months since. But now, here, face to face with him, it was as if every one of her senses woke up truly for the first time since October 2019. Her heart pounded just like it had when their hands had touched, her eyes honed in on every detail of his face in the same way it had the moment his sunglasses had come off, and her hands thrummed with the desire to reach out and touch that soft, smooth skin yet again —the only man she wanted to touch, if she were being completely honest with herself. Just as before, every cell in her body pulled her toward him, and she couldn't turn down the magnet's power one little bit.

Nick's laugh, which had set her spinning in the first place, ultimately brought her back to Earth. This time it was the sound of his surprise—a shockingly high-pitched yawlp for a six-foot two, two hundred-pound octogenarian and the result of whatever joke she'd just entirely missed. Munie used it as a life raft and forcibly ripped her eyes from Jack's to return Nick's merriment with a chuckle of her own.

"Drink, baby?" he asked with tears of hilarity running down his face.

"Absolutely. Thanks Nick. Scotch rocks, please."

"I got it, Bo." Jack's voice was right beside her now, rolling into her ear like warm honey. "It's your hand." He gestured with a small movement of his arm toward the card table, and the faint waft of his scent —cocoa butter and the clean, pheromonic pull of Farella—made her sway on her feet.

His gaze was locked back on hers again, this time from a foot away. She could see the still-youthful smoothness of his skin, the shine in his eyes. In slow motion, that unforgettable grin unfurled across a lush, delicious mouth as he beckoned her, his dimples dropping right to her belly. She was a string long silent, now being strummed once again. "Let's go," was all he said.

He held out his hand to her, but their fingers didn't have time to touch, as much as hers may have been aching for the renewed contact.

"Now hold on just a second there, Jackie. Don't think your ass is getting out of here without my birthday song!"

"Jackie?" she quipped with a quirk of her eyebrow. He simply lifted a corner of his lips in response, dimple flaring and eyes dancing, as he kept up the banter without missing a beat.

"Oh come on," he retorted to Nickles, "you know I got you. I just need a little time to catch up with your film making partner here—it's been a long, long while." His words were simple, but the expression on his face as he looked at her was anything but. Even so, Munie kept a serene smile on her lips as Jack brought his hand to the small of her back, out of Nickles' view. The familiar feel of his warm palm there sent shock waves up and down her spine.

"Well OK, but you hold him to it then, baby girl, OK?" Nickles instructed to Munie with a laugh.

"My pleasure, Nick," she replied, her calm exterior belying a downright woozy interior. Where was that damned drink?

As if on cue, Jack applied the faintest of caresses against her lumbar spine and gently ushered her toward the the back of the house and Nickles' enormous kitchen.

"Oh shit," she breathed, taking in the top-shelf surroundings. The space was taken up by no fewer than three islands, each one set with a spread of exquisite catered food. A fully-stocked bar off to the right and a wood-burning fireplace crackling right in the center of the room completed the mind-blowing, *Architectural Digest*-level picture.

"I know." Jack grabbed two glasses from the bar and began dropping in ice. Clink. Clink. Clink. Clink. The cubes hit the rocks glasses with the same high, urgent rhythm as her heart as she watched his strong hands move back and forth with the ice tongs. This was uncharted territory. If the previous five minutes were any indication, staying objective and unemotional was not going to be a feat for the faint-hearted, even if it was absolutely necessary.

She should walk away. She had to walk away. It was imperative that she separate herself from the situation. But regardless of how many miles her intellectual mind was telling her to place between herself and Jack, her body simply wouldn't oblige. Her feet wouldn't budge from their spot next to him. Her ears wanted his voice, her fingers wanted his touch, her nose wanted that fragrance, and her eyes? They were already heading back home.

She let her gaze move upward slowly from his hands, taking him in. The sunglasses were gone, his face clean shaven. The dense, dark coils of his hair were now well-managed in a neat, orderly cut. He wore a cream-colored button-down shirt, rolled to the elbows; she could see the muscles of his forearms twisting and flexing as he squeezed a lime quarter into his glass, animating his tattoos as he moved. Light gray slacks and loafers completed the attire. Simple, no frills. No bling either, she noted—just a silver ring on his left middle finger and a simple gold chain around his neck.

He caught her looking, and pegged her with a sidelong glance that quickly turned into another full-on Jack-and-Munie stare. It was a skill they'd perfected, as easy and right as slipping on a warm wool mitten. There they stayed, still as statues, reading libraries in each other's eyes, until ...

"Oh no it is NOT!" The bubble broke suddenly as a young man strode into the kitchen. "He lives! Gene Coltrane lives!"

He clapped Jack loudly on the back, causing him to reluctantly tear his gaze from Munie's in order to deliver an equally violent, back-patting Dude Hug.

"Good to see you, brother."

"Amazing to see you, Gene! Damn, man, it must be at least two years since I've laid eyes on you in person anywhere. How've you been? You look great. Truly."

"I'm good. Real good. Damon, I want you to meet Rai Paley. Rai, this is Damon Chau. Damon's a phenomenal sound engineer. We've worked together off and on for years." Munie warmed from tip to toes; he was using her professional name.

He'd kept her secret. He'd kept *their* secret.

Damon exhibited roughly the same level of excitement as a puppy on a sugar high. "Wait, whoa!" he exclaimed, only slightly less loudly than before, eyes wide. "You did Nick's documentary, right?"

"I did." She smiled softly.

"Damn! Bravo. It was excellent—really amazing work."

Munie knew he was right, but she blushed anyway. "Thank you, Damon. He made my job easy. Nick's the best."

As uber-aware as she already was of Jack's presence so close to her, she turned to peek at him anyway. He was smiling at her with eyes full of genuine pride. "She's amazing," was all he said, not to Damon but to her, as he drank in the details of her face.

"And you, bro," Damon continued, wagging a finger in Jack's face. "You do know that new song is pissing off every songwriter in Hollywood, right? Didn't it just hit platinum last week?"

Jack looked down shyly and wiped his thumb and index finger down the sides of his mouth. He was shy now? Munie was baffled. "Yeah, it did."

"And you realize Nick won't let you out of here tonight until you play it, right?"

Jack just laughed. "Yeah, I got that already. Direct order."

Damon grabbed his drink and waved it in the air. "Just be lucky he didn't ask you to play the whole damn album! That thing is fire, brother. I'm serious."

Jack's gaze went to Munie as he replied, a sweet smile on his lips. "Well, when inspiration strikes, right?"

It was a sentiment too subtle for Damon to catch, but it landed right in the middle of Munie's chest. Feeling flushed and a little too warm, she excused herself to head over to the hors d'oeuvres spread on the main island, leaving the two men to catch up.

Inhale, exhale.

Staring at the hummus, she willed her heart to stop hammering in her chest. Being face-to-face with Jack again had knocked her completely and totally off balance. Even if she'd known, had time to mentally prepare, it would have rocked her. But this? *Breathe, Munie,* she repeated silently to herself.

Everything was just as electric as she remembered, but exponentially stronger. The urge to touch him was almost unbearable, as hard to manage as the mere act of being near him, his voice, his energy, his eyes. Him. Jack.

Why did he have to be here? She willed the avocado puffs to answer her, but they refused. She'd spent two and a half years compartmentalizing her experiences of Jack into something she could navigate. Though he was still a permanent resident in her mind, she had just begun to get more nimble in drawing the proverbial drapes now and then. She worked in different circles than he did. She deliberately chose not to follow his public comings and goings. She made an effort (successfully until now) to dodge events that he may be attending. It had been working. Her plan had been to progress ultimately to a space of blissful indifference, where she could throw open those drapes anytime at all with nary a thought of him. But now? Now it had all just spontaneously combusted with the mere sound of his—

"Hungry?"

His voice was low, intimate, wafting into her ear from right behind her. An arm came out to her right, inches from her skin, aiming for the serving dishes on the counter in front of her. She watched him pick up a strawberry with those beautiful, light brown fingers and place it gently on her empty plate. "I am," he cooed.

Another reach, this time his body pressing gently against hers from behind with a familiar pressure, his front fit perfectly to her back, all warmth and solidness. One of the traitorous avocado puffs now rested on the plate next to the strawberry.

The next time he pushed closer to her, he didn't even bother with the guise of reaching for food. He reached for her instead, his hand trailing lightly up and down her arm, his breath at her ear, body flush against hers. There they stayed, bathing in each other's energy, their body heat once again melding to make fire. No one spoke until more footsteps signaled another impending intruder into their space.

"We should talk," she said quietly to the air in front of her.

"Yeah," agreed the voice in her ear, followed by one more maddeningly soft caress of his fingers down her arm, then his body's sudden separation from hers. She felt the cold lack of him immediately, until his hand wrapped around hers and she felt that familiar pulse coursing down her arm like a returning friend. "Out back—this way."

Munie let him guide her out the kitchen door and into the garden beyond, a drink in her left hand and a mystery in her right.

Songs on this Track

Bring It On Home to Me: Lyrics and music by Sam Cooke; performed by Sam Cooke

20

———

NAKED

"You look good, Jack."

They were sitting on a porch swing in Nickles' back yard, nursing their drinks—her whiskey and his seltzer with lime.

He smiled, maybe a bit shyly. "Thanks."

"No, I mean it. You look strong, healthy, more ... sturdy."

"I got a damn personal trainer. I love him, but he's a real asshole."

"An asshole bearing gifts."

"Ha! Yeah. Now I got a two-pack. Something to tell my mama."

It was easy just sitting there together, letting the night sounds tell all the truths their mouths weren't ready to share. Like plugging a cord into an outlet, Munie simply soaked in the renewed current running between them, something she hadn't felt since they'd walked out the doors of the Bellweather Hotel in Studio City, headed in opposite directions, all words gone. Now it was different; now there were a lot of words to say, but none that were necessary just yet. The words would churn up everything; the quiet was peaceful, and she was happy to savor just a bit more of it.

She looked out into the night, past Nickles' pool, past the land-scaped garden, and toward the hills beyond, then slowly panned back to take in her companion's profile. Where she'd noticed circles under his eyes two years ago, there were none now. Where his skin had been slightly mottled then, it was smooth and supple now, maybe a touch darker from the sun. He looked both younger and older, haler and more mature, abiding quietly within himself as they swayed gently back and forth, one of his feet levering on the stone porch floor to power them.

She smiled and exhaled a tiny, airy chuckle; he turned toward the sound, toward her, his face becoming her horizon.

"What is it?" His smile was a gentle lift of his lips, his voice soft.

"I was just thinking about 'Singapore Street.'" She indicated the swing in which they were sitting. "How completely wrong I was. '*Rocking, rocking.*' Egad."

His smile broadened, shoulders shaking the tiniest bit in amusement. "Shocked you, did I?"

"A little ... which made me mad. I don't normally miss double entendre."

"Maybe that's the nice thing about it—you get what you want to get. And you got the romance."

He simply looked at her, and she looked at him. "I guess so."

A few more moments passed in silence, the only sound the gentle creak of the swing and the distant tinkle of the fountain at the far end of Nickles' pool. Jack took her hand and gently interlaced their fingers, both of them gazing at this quiet, peaceful union of their bodies.

He spoke to their hands, rubbing his thumb gently over her skin. "Did you see it?"

She let out a sigh and closed her eyes, savoring his touch. "Yes."

"You didn't reach out."

"I didn't know what to do. You have no idea what that speech... and that performance... did to me."

He looked up at her with earnest, patient eyes. "So tell me."

"I don't know where to start."

"Just start with whatever is in that beautiful head right now."

She took in this flesh-and-blood source of her exquisite emotional ache. His expression was devoid of any subtext, as though the only thing he wanted in the entire world was to understand what was on her heart. So she told him.

"I couldn't sleep for three weeks after the interview."

"Me neither. Longer. Say more."

"Before, I thought I had everything figured out. I was good with work and life and... shit, Jack... I was happy. Then I left you that day and there was a big hole wherever you weren't."

There was silence for a moment, then his barely perceptible sigh and nod of the head. "Yeah."

She laughed. It was a humorless, pinched sound. "I didn't do interviews for four months after Studio City. I couldn't focus. So I moved into research, editing, all the things that didn't remind me as much of you."

"But you got the article out."

"Barely. Do you have any idea how fucking difficult it was for me to be objective? I mean, for goodness sake, I talk about how you smell! In a journalistic piece!" Her voice began to pitch higher; she pulled her hand from his in order to cross her arms, an effort to contain the ire starting to bubble up from where it had lain dormant for so long, covered in sadness.

"You're angry. I don't blame you. And you probably want to ask a lot of things. So ask."

She stood, needing to get a little bit of distance from him. "Of course I'm angry, Jack! Why the hell wouldn't I be? I spend two years —two entire years—of my life trying to sew myself back together after you ripped my heart open that day in Studio City, only to have you pull out the stitches on national TV before they're even healed? Why? What possible good does that do?"

Furious as she was, Jack's continued composure just added fuel to the fire. Where was his temper? Where were the wildly gesticulating arms she'd seen repeatedly the last time they went toe-to-toe like this? The sarcasm? Its absence was sending her even further into the embers. She wheeled over to where he sat and clamped her hands on the wooden back of the swing, bracketing his torso as she bore down on him.

"Say something, damnit. React. Swear. Something. I have a lot of questions? Damn straight. Here's a question, Jack. Why the hell didn't you just find me and talk to me sometime during the last two and a half years instead of making some massive pronouncement during the *American Music Awards*, of all places? It's not like I was on fucking Mars!"

He looked up at her, nose to nose, and responded with an infuriatingly level tone. "Because I was almost dead at the bottom of the well, Munie."

She stepped away, thunderstruck.

The silence that followed was deafening. At length, Munie walked down the stairs into the garden, facing the night. No one spoke for several more minutes but the crickets. Finally, from his seat on the swing, Jack continued in the same calm, resigned voice.

"I said those things because they were true. Every word. What you told me in Studio City stung. And that pain, plus being in love with you and losing you... it all just sent me right over the edge. But I had to hear it."

She heard the ice in his glass clink softly as he took a drink, and the clunk as he set it back down on the table. And though she couldn't see him, she just knew he was sighing and running a hand through his hair. She could see it clear as day behind her own closed eyes.

Finally, she heard him rise.

"Can I come over? Please?"

She nodded in silence, her gaze still on the horizon, and without looking back, she could feel him approach behind her. Then his voice was right next to her again. He reached out to stroke her arm as he spoke, and she reflexively leaned into his touch. "You hurt me but you reached me. You changed me. Does that make sense?"

"I have no idea," she half-laughed, her head swimming. "But damnit, Jack—I was right here."

He kissed her shoulder gently. "You gotta understand, I was in a really fragile place for a long time. I didn't leave the house until almost the end of 2020. And by then I figured you'd written me off, or found another man—"

She laughed again, the sound just as humorless as before, but now with a bitter tang on the finish. "Find another man? Are you delusional?"

She heard his words come out with more bite this time. "Fucking hell, Munie. You still don't see, do you? Look at me. Please, damnit." He took hold of her elbow, guiding her to face him. She was shocked to see tear tracks on both of his cheeks.

"Jack ..." She looked at him, his honest face and guileless eyes, but then she truly *looked* at him, standing before her naked, vulnerable. It was at that moment that she registered what he'd said just minutes before.

He was in love with her.

The crickets were deafening.

He brought a hand out to stroke her face. "Call me weak, or cowardly, but I was scared to death that you'd reject me, and I knew that kind of hurt would send me right back down the drain. But at the same time, I couldn't keep it inside. So I wrote it in music. Munie— you're the album. You're the entire fucking thing."

Although somewhere deep down, she already knew, hearing the confession from Jack himself was an emotional tidal wave. These songs were the deepest, most stripped-down, most soulful pieces he'd ever written. She'd been in tears the first and only time she'd had the fortitude to play the album through. Now she knew for sure—those songs were for her. She was Jack's inspiration. Munie couldn't find words, so she just brought a hand to his cheek; he closed his eyes against her touch and turned to kiss the inside of her palm, then smiled ironically.

"But even that wasn't enough. Did you ever feel something so powerful that you just had to get it out? Even if I couldn't get to you like this, like we are now, I had to tell you what I had to say somehow. So that's why I did it at the awards show. Sometimes the truth is easier for me to say onstage—that's just how I am. I figured I'd just let it go, and if it landed, it landed." His gaze drifted down, then back into her waiting eyes. "I couldn't tell you in person, but I couldn't not say it. At least, that's where I was then."

She took in a long, shaky inhale. "Where are you now?" she whispered.

"Now I'm right here watching God and the universe and 'ole Nick Boone step in." He placed a delicate kiss on her forehead, his lips turning up at the corners as he leaned back to look at her. The lightness of his comment was like a cool compress on a hot day, and she was so grateful for it that she decided to keep it going.

"Nice setup—'God, the universe and Nickles Boone walk into a bar.'"

His face froze for a split second as the joke sank in, and then he laughed out loud. It was like he had been so weighed down with words that the real Jack hadn't been able to shine through, but now the veneer had cracked, and it was like seeing the first ray of sunshine on a spring morning. With a grin of her own, she began to walk slowly down the path through the garden, Jack falling into step beside her, his shoulders still shaking with giggles.

"But seriously, Jack, what are God, the universe, and Nick all in cahoots about?"

He wiped his eyes and exhaled, giggling again. "What are cahoots?"

"It's just an expression. In other words, what are they all up to together?"

Giggle fits controlled, he looked back at her with a sly smile. "Conspiring for us to be doing this tonight."

"How so?"

"Don't think I haven't been following you, girl."

"Oh yeah?"

"Absolutely. I'm your personal stalker." Another grin, and there was a dimple. Jack was back.

"Following me to the post office and the dentist?" She weaved her arm through his, like a Victorian couple on a courting stroll.

"Although that would be pretty fucking exciting, no. I kept tabs on your work."

"Really?"

"Yeah. You're a talented damn woman, you know that?"

"I do."

"Good."

"But I still don't see what this has to do with God, the universe, or Nick."

"I read that you were going to be doing his doc."

She nodded. "We started talking about it in July of 2020, during quarantine. We did as much remotely as we could, and then started filming as soon as things opened back up. It was a long process." She stopped, turning to face him. "But it was a gift, Jack. A real gift. Like a lifeline. I needed that work to get me back on track again."

He sighed wearily and kissed her hand. "I'm so, so sorry."

"It's wasn't just you," she replied quickly. "It was both of us. We both left things the way we did."

"True."

She turned back onto the path and took his arm again. "Keep going. You knew about the doc. Then what?"

"So then two weeks ago, Nick invites me to his birthday party. We got really close while I was under it —we're family now." He chuckled. "My crazy, pain in the ass Uncle Bo."

She giggled. "You know, sometimes when he smiles like he does, I kind of think he looks like Cab Calloway."

Jack cackled again. "I can see him coming at me now." He puffed out his chest and pulled a face shockingly similar to Nickles', his inflection perfect. "'*Hi-de-hi-de-hi-de-hi*,' asshole."

Munie laughed loud and deep; Jack swiveled around suddenly to face her. "Oh fuck I've missed that sound," he whispered. His eyes were shining and alive as they took her in.

"You're off topic," she whispered back in an effort not to kiss him right there and then.

He just grinned, not moving. They had come to a stop under a massive oak tree intricately strung with fairy lights; the reflection bounced off Jack's face, his eyes, and their now-joined hands, making everything dazzle.

"I knew you two would be tight now," he continued. "Bo mentions you a lot. So I knew he'd invite you. And damnit, woman, I hoped like hell you'd be here. I figured that if this thing we have is as meant to be as it feels, as it's always felt, you'd come, and I'd get the chance to do what I should have done a long time ago. So here I am, Munie, right here, right now, using this gift that God and the universe are giving me."

She turned her head away, tears threatening.

"Look at me." He placed a hand on her chin, delicately turning her gaze back to his, and brought his face so close to hers that she could smell the lime still lingering on his lips. His expression was serene but resolute, as if he was damn sight going to get every word out into the open air for her to see.

"It's you. It's all you, and that's all it's been since the day I met you. I haven't seen another woman, I haven't thought about another woman ... I haven't touched another woman for over two years. I haven't wanted to. You're it. Raimunda Penelope Paley, I love you. Know that's true."

He caught her tears with his thumbs as he continued to speak, even as his own eyes began to fill. His voice came more quietly now, gentle and raw. "And I leave that at your feet. I believe you feel the same, that this energy right here is us forever, but that's for you to decide, in your time. I'll be here. I'll be waiting for you."

With that, he tilted his head to the side and brought his mouth to hers in a soft, slow kiss. Munie's entire world stopped in that moment and there was only him, only Jack, only the beautiful alchemy of their bodies together. Kissing him was so much more than she remembered, and she allowed herself to get lost in the sensations of him for those precious few seconds. When he pulled back to look at her, he was smiling gently.

All the air in the world was in the space between them; it was too much. "Anything else?" she whispered, desperate to divert herself from the truth right in front of her. The back door opened suddenly into the silence that followed, Nickles' booming voice breaking the spell.

"Jackie, where the hell you at? You owe me a birthday song, damnit, and I ain't getting any younger over here."

She watched Jack's smile deepen, his dimples waking up as he called out a response over his shoulder. "Hold your pants on, Minnie the Moocher, I'll be there in a minute."

"I ain't got enough ass left to keep 'em up," Nickles retorted, then turned back into the house, continuing to mutter under his breath. "Minnie the Moocher. I'll give him Minnie the Moocher, the tired-ass son of a bitch." The door clanged shut behind him.

Munie and Jack burst into laughter.

"He totally loves you."

"Obviously," Jack agreed, shoulders shaking. She watched his smile slowly move from overt to subtle as his gaze fell back on her.

"One more thing," he continued, bending to whisper in her ear. "I want to be inside you so bad I can barely stand here right now." He kissed her earlobe, gently sucking the flesh into his mouth, and let out a low groan, making Munie so dizzy she had to grab onto his elbow for support. Placing his forehead against hers, he gave her just two more whispered words. "Your turn." With that, he simply turned and walked back into the house.

Munie didn't move for some time. Was it minutes? Was it hours? It seemed that time moved on a different revolution before and after this interchange. Yes, she'd thought of him every day since 2019. Yes, his words at the awards broadcast had pulled at her from the root. Yes, she wanted him on a level deeper than she could comprehend— both body and soul.

But the realization that she truly *loved* him came to her as she walked into Nickles' house and joined the swell of people around the piano, all watching Gene Coltrane serve up a stunning, delicate rendition of his new platinum hit "Naked," the song he had written expressly and solely for her.

Songs on this Track

Minnie the Moocher: Songwriters Cab Calloway, Irving Mills, and Clarence Gaskill; performed by Cab Calloway

21

———————

THE FIRST TIME

July 2022
Glenys MacKenzie's House, London, UK

There wasn't enough chamomile in the world.

Munie played back the moments at Nickles' house over and over again, a sad song on loop. Her outburst, Jack's confession, the kiss, his song—and the moment she turned away from the piano and walked out the front door without looking back. She could see him as clearly as if he were still standing next to her in Nickles' kitchen. She could feel him as surely as if his lips were still mingled with hers. His whispered voice echoed in her ear over and over again. "Your turn."

So passed the first week. And the second. And the third. And Munie Paley still quite frankly had no idea what to do. It was as though her body had moved into a state of almost complete inertia. She ate absently, walked aimlessly, stared at the TV without even noticing what the hell was on the screen.

She loved him, yes. But. But what?

Something was stopping her. Some invisible obstacle was blocking her way. But she could no more identify what it was then she could lasso the moon. So she studied her experience of Jack Flores in the event that some nugget of a "why" would magically appear before her eyes, elucidate the entire situation, and give voice and rationale to her fear.

Wait. Fear? She tested the word again in her mind. Yes. Fear. *OK, Munie,* she said to herself, *now we have an interview. What are you afraid of?*

There were red flags all over the place: drugs, sleeping around, multiple kids with multiple women that he didn't even have relationships with. An arrest thrown in there for good measure.

And, of course, always hovering in the back of her mind, an unscratchable itch, was one simple fact. He hadn't remembered her.

Plus, he'd been easily moved to anger during their interview, though that part of him had seemed quiet at Nick's party. But still...

He was reckless, impulsive, unpredictable. Passionate.

Passionate. Ardent. Soulful. Intelligent. Challenging. Genuine and fierce in how he cared. Unwavering in how he loved.

In how he loved her.

She was miserable.

And so, three weeks and four days after Jack professed his love to her in Nick Boone's back yard, she found herself sitting at the table in Glenys' London breakfast nook, staring morosely into an excellent cup of Earl Grey.

"My darling," Glenys comforted in an unusually soft tone, her hand on Munie's arm, "I love you dearly, but I've no idea how to help you at the moment. You need to meet me halfway here." Glenys' concern was clear in her utter absence of wit or typical snarky commentary. "Tell me again what he said."

Munie rested her weary head in her hands, willing the images to stop spinning.

"He said I basically turned his life around, he loves me, wrote that raw, honest album entirely because of me. Doesn't want any other woman but me."

"And you believe he's sincere?"

"Completely."

Though most friends would challenge such a quick response in similar situations, Glenys knew Munie, and knew that her gut, however twisted with melancholy it was at the moment, was never wrong when it came to people.

"And you?" she whispered, if only to allow her friend to hear her own words spoken into the air, for the contents of her heart were crystal clear.

"Glenys, I think I fell in love with him in the first five minutes we were together." She sighed and shook her head, her next words a whisper into the air. "Every time."

Munie recalled the moment a young Jack had first smiled at her in the record store, thawing something that had been long frozen inside her. She thought back to the heavy magnetic charge of their first glance at the *Theta* mixer years later. She relived the moment Gene Coltrane had removed his sunglasses during that damned interview in Studio City, and she'd fallen even further into the deep trueness of Jack's eyes—the moment she first saw home, and saw the same sentiment reflected back on her.

"Then Munie, why not be with him? You're the wisest woman I've ever known, so clearly there must be a reason."

She thought for several seconds, not coming up with anything. It was like trying to capture moonlight in a jar. No ideas came to her; no salient words made their way out of her mouth. Instead, Glenys' Pokemon-shaped kitchen radio did the talking for her as an inordinately beautiful George Michael cover of 'The First Time Ever I Saw Your Face' wafted rudely into the room. *Great timing, George.* Munie just dropped her forehead onto the table with a groan and an audible thunk.

The words "why not?" colored the rest of her week in London, as she and Glenys walked arm in arm down the summer streets, as they noshed on curry and pints in Glenys' favorite local pub, and as they sat on benches at the Tate, Munie looking at masterpieces but not really seeing anything.

The friends had worked through each red flag in turn, dismantling them one by one:

He was an addict, but now he's sober. Could he relapse? Yes, but that's not it.

He was a womanizer, but he vows to be hers only. Could he be unfaithful? Yes, but he could also be true. That's not it.

He's all over the world all the time—no schedule, no dependability. But given Munie's historically independent lifestyle, that was actually more of a check in the "plus" box.

He's a musician and she's a music journalist. Conflict? At this point in her career, Munie was too well-established to care. Not it.

The decision came during an ice cream break outside Westminster Abbey on the last day of her visit, a perfectly sunny Saturday. It was Glenys whose words sealed the deal.

"Mun," she offered in a matter-of-fact tone with vanilla dotting the corner of her mouth, "if this were a professional project, and you couldn't find your answer, what would you do?"

"Keep thinking. Keep researching."

"Bullshit. You'd talk to as many people as you had to in order to get the real deal, yes, but then you'd tap into your gut. I've seen you do it. You turn off your huge brain and turn on that ridiculously accurate emotional divining rod. You feel for the full story. Do that for yourself. Stop thinking and just feel." With that, Glenys pulled out her phone to show Munie the screenshot she'd taken that morning:

The 2022 Curaçao Jazz Festival

August 11-14

Four days of jazz greatness, featuring headliners Lester Day and his Band, Pongo Purdy, Gene Coltrane, and The Marle Family

Munie handed back the phone with a resigned sigh and took a lick of her ice cream. It was time. She had to do something, and this was as good a something as she'd find. "Well, Glen, as they say around here, 'needs must,' right?"

"As they say in America, Mun, 'abso-fucking-lutely.'"

————————————————————————

Curaçao, August 2022

· · ·

AN ANCILLARY BENEFIT to both loving what you do and being a self-proclaimed workaholic is that you rarely feel the need to take time off. Therefore, when Munie decided to take another ten days of personal leave so shortly her London excursion, it was still a mere dribble out of the giant vat of her amassed PTO. Plus, given the effusiveness of her HR rep's good-holiday wishes, she had a feeling she was also doing a solid for the corporate wellbeing agenda.

But on the flip side, when one rarely takes vacation, it's hard to turn off the brain. As she sat on the sand behind her Curaçao rental, the cool grains tickling between her toes, she found the inability of her brain to 'can it' to be remarkable, indeed.

Another phone check—nothing yet. Micah, who now covered the jazz festival for *Lift*, had committed to letting her know as soon as there was a solid schedule in place, but festivals were notorious scheduling nightmares, especially when they were outdoors, so who knew? Well enough.

It would have been easy to just call Jack and tell him she was here —she had his number, after all—but her gut told her not to. Somehow, that approach smacked of too much premeditation, and Munie wanted their next interaction to be just as organic as all the others had been, at least on his part. Especially given their history, she wanted to see his exact reaction when he saw her, to observe precisely how she affected him when it came right down to it. No preparation, no rehearsal—all the way live.

She tucked her phone back in her pocket and took a walk along the stunning white sand beach, following placid, sky-blue water as far as the eye could see—the calm before the predicated storm that was meant to roll on through like a truck tomorrow. Rather than staying at yet another hotel, she had opted for a sleek but adorable shanty-style beach house a few miles from the main town. Quiet. Serene. She could think here. She could cook for herself, sit on the patio overlooking the ocean, and just regroup.

Her plan was to find Jack and talk with him—that's as far as she'd gotten. What would happen from there was a mystery even to her. But there had to be a starting point, and it finally flashed onto her screen the following morning as she sipped her coffee, in the form of a text message from Micah:

> Soundcheck was yesterday. Coltrane on tonight 8-9:30 pm, then a reception for him at the Sovereign 11 pm-1 am. Let me know if you want access.

Shit, shit, shit. It would have been much easier to get a quiet moment with Jack at soundcheck versus backstage before the show, amid all the hubbub. It was a more controlled environment, quieter, easier to navigate. Performance night could promise absolutely nothing. As she reread Micah's note, the delicately-managed anxiety that had been simmering under the surface of Munie's skin since she'd first decided to make this trip suddenly began oozing through her pores, running through her veins, constricting her lungs. Her breath sped up. Her heart raced.

There were options. She could just call it a day, go home, and regroup, putting away the problem for another time. But as she looked out at the placid sea that was the antithesis of her inner angst, she realized there would be no such calm for her until she faced Jack again, until she made peace with this relationship one way or another. She was scared witless to take the step, to open Pandora's box, but she was just as afraid not to. Whether such a feat could be accomplished during this trip, she had no idea, but she was going to try nonetheless. She had to.

By the time she had Ubered the long, slow four miles of local road to the concert venue that evening, everything was in chaos. The coming storm had reconfigured schedules abysmally, and Jack was nowhere to be seen in the thirty minutes before he was due onstage. All Munie could do was take her seat in the second row (thanks, Micah), umbrella in hand, and wait.

She could barely sit still, but didn't trust her legs to stand. She was counting the seconds until showtime, but was dreading the moment the music started, when she'd see her love and anguish reflected clearly in the bright stage lights. Not knowing how she would feel upon seeing him up there scared her perhaps most of all.

And how would Jack even respond? She was walking right into his professional world with no advance notice. How would he feel about that? And beyond his surprise, would he welcome her back into his orbit, or had he taken her silence as rejection and moved on? He'd said it was her turn, but was her turn ... over?

It was time to find out. Jack walked onstage in white linen pants and a blue short-sleeved linen shirt, his saxophone around his neck, and her heart immediately began to thrum against her rib cage as if anticipating the beat of the first song. He waved out to the middle of the crowd, smiling happily, and she immediately began to feel that prickle behind her eyes.

He didn't notice her; his eyes were closed as he played, so she could take time to savor him unseen. The muscles in his forearms flexed just so as he pressed the valves of his instrument. His body language was loose and relaxed as he flowed back and forth in time with the music, as comfortable as if he were just strolling in the park. It was beautiful to watch.

Just as she was becoming hypnotized by the dance of his fingers and the music they made, he let the sax rest in its collar against his chest, placed a hand on the standing mike, and began to sing.

And Munie began to cry. Hard.

Every deep longing she'd ever had bubbled to the surface, given voice by Jack's perfectly real and clear tenor. Her urges, wants, insecurities, vulnerabilities—everything over which she had no control—all pushed to the surface at once like a tidal wave. It was this feeling, she suddenly realized, that was her block. Munie knew as she gazed, helplessly in love, at the man on the stage, that to give in to her feelings would be to let go, to free fall with no way to steer, slow down, or even understand where she was going.

And that concept scared the hell out of her. It was too much to ask. She was holding onto the rope for dear life, and the thought of letting go, or even loosening her grip just a little, was inconceivable. She couldn't do it.

She had to get out of there before she had a panic attack. Still weeping, she turned in all directions to find a path through the thick throng of now-standing people around and behind her. She felt locked in, trapped, and the panic grew, making her movements more and more frantic. Jack must have perceived the commotion in Row Two out of the corner of his eye, because he turned his head and looked directly at her just before she could retreat into the crowd, an expression of utter disbelief transforming his face.

They stared at each other for a few long seconds. He missed the next two lines of the song. She turned on her heel and fled.

Songs on this Track

The First Time Ever I Saw Your Face: Lyrics and music by Ewan MacColl; performed by George Michael.

22

TAKE THE MOON

August 2022
Curaçao

THE THUNDER, THE LIGHTNING, AND THE TORRENTIAL RAIN WERE Munie's partners that night as she huddled on the couch in her beachfront rental, hours after having run crying from the concert. It was as if the Earth's floodgates and her own had opened in tandem, the heavy raindrops mirroring her teardrops as she sat on the sofa hugging her knees and weeping with abandon. The walls were down, the levee had broken, and there was nothing she could do but just feel it all.

This kind of love was too heavy, too overwhelming for her to carry. But still, she felt the loss of him in every pore of her body, like a promise made and then taken away. Her heart ached in a way she could never remember experiencing, almost as if a literal knife were twisting inside her chest, rending the muscle asunder. She placed her hand on the spot in an effort to somehow contain the pain, to restrict it. But it just kept hurting.

She'd leave tomorrow. That's what she had to do. Her mind screamed at her to go home and regroup, get some objectivity and safe space so that she could take back control. But her heart was at war with common sense, screaming just as loudly to be allowed to truly fall in love and feel it in every pore, even if it was too big for her to rein in. The warring of heart and mind ripped at her, fueling her tears like a personal rain cloud. As she listened to the thunder crack over her head, she recognized that, try as she might, there was only one medicine that could possibly heal the ache that reverberated throughout her body and soul. The realization landed like a boulder, making her sob even harder.

A knock at the door. Another, louder. Then a voice, it's urgency competing with the rage of the storm. "Munie! Let me in!"

There was only one voice that was so firmly etched in her brain—and that was the one.

She opened the door to find Jack standing in the pouring rain, his sopping linen shirt in his hand and an unfathomable expression on his face.

"Why did you come?" he demanded. Panting and breathless, he was almost shouting in an effort to be heard over the torrent of water cascading down the stooped porch roof. His eyes simultaneously bored into hers and traveled over her body, taking in her rain-wrinkled sundress, the smallness of her bare feet against the tile floor, her beautiful face flushed and wet with tears.

"How did you find me?" Munie's voice was small and shaky, even to her own ear.

"Why did you come?" he repeated, more loudly this time. His sleeveless undershirt was sticking to him in splotchy patches as water continued to blow all around him, his bare shoulders shiny with wetness, but he didn't notice or care. For a solid five seconds, there was only the sound of the pounding rain, accentuated by a distant rumble of thunder.

Only truth was here, Munie realized as she stared back at him. It was her why, her sole motivation not just for this trip, but for everything else, too.

"I came here for you."

She watched as her words caused a flood of emotion to cascade across his face. There were now tears in his eyes as he looked at her, plaintively, needfully, and hopelessly in love.

"Then why did you leave? And why did you leave Nick's party without saying goodbye? You can't just ..." He stopped talking and let his head drop, emotion overtaking him. "You're killing me, Munie." When he looked back up at her, he was crying.

Her only answer was silence, accompanied by the insistent pounding of the rain. She stood at the threshold of the cottage, one foot in the safety of a world she knew and could navigate, and the other on the precipice of something terrifying for both its mystery and its undeniable pull. Impossibly strong. Impossibly right.

"Say something, damnit!" he shouted, his eyes both pleading and demanding.

There was too much inside her to contain; her words thundered as the thunder boomed, tears once again warming her cheeks.

"What do you want me to say, Jack? Do you want me to say I'm sorry, or I'm afraid, or that all of this is way too much to handle? What the fuck do you want to hear from me?"

His eyes were lasers, boring into her. "The truth, Munie. That's it. Just give me the fucking truth. If it means I turn around and walk out of your life tonight, then so be it. But woman, know that it would be only because you tell me to. I want you. Period. It's like that. But you have to want me, too. Where are you, Munie? Just fucking TELL ME!" He paused and took a deep breath to check his temper before continuing in a softer tone. "What are you afraid of?"

Her heart hammered in her chest, and the words poured out of her aching soul. "Why should I believe you? Why wouldn't I be exactly like all those others—and all those other me's, for that matter? Out of sight, out of mind. Tell me you love me now, then walk out the door and that's it. Just like you said in the interview. I can't do that, Jack. I won't."

He took one step toward the threshold, hands gripping either side of the door frame, and she took a step back. His face was a picture of determination now; her heart was blowing in the wind.

"I had more to say before you left me on that balcony in Studio

City. You didn't give me the chance." He looked deeply into her eyes, his voice thick with significance. "It was my turn."

"Jack—"

"No. Listen. You're right—I didn't remember you from Laurel Canyon or Nick's fucking pizza place. I do remember it all now, but that's not enough. I should have then. And I didn't. That's on me. There's a reason, and I get what that is now, but I'm still an absolute asshole for it." The rain just kept coming; even though water blew sideways and continued to wet his hair, skin, and clothes, he didn't budge from the spot. "But I still knew you as soon as I laid eyes on you in Studio City."

He took another step forward, and this time she didn't back away. "You were the same woman who walked into that record store when I was twenty-two, who let me hold her in the back room when she was crying, who melted me to the fucking floor when she kissed me. Her hair was dark brown, her eyes were green with flecks of gold in them ... and her name was Munie."

She let out a choked exhale. Words were beginning to form in her mind, but she didn't have time to get any of them out.

"That woman left and never came back. Never reached out again. It hit me here—" Jack took Munie's hand and placed it on his chest— "and it hit me hard. She was my first love." His eyes began to fill again as he continued to speak, his confession pouring out of him like the rivulets of water down the roof.

"When you walked into that interview suite, the... shit... the way of you was familiar. Then you laughed, and I recognized that too. But when you looked in my eyes and gave me your name, that's when I knew. Munie. My Munie." He looked into the distance, then turned back to her with pain written all over his face. "I loved you then, from the first time I heard you laugh at that damned album cover. And I love you now—so fucking much. I never stopped." He wiped hastily at his eyes, then locked his gaze solidly onto hers, his voice an impassioned whisper. "Woman, take the moon, my life, and everything in it —just tell me you love me back."

Munie shook her head slowly to clear it and looked away into the storm, the night made blurry by her tears. Jack leaned forward a few inches, coming closer to her orbit. His voice came to her more softly this time. "Stop running, Munie. Say the words. Please," he whispered. As she moved her gaze back to his, she saw his need for her more clearly than he could have ever conveyed with language.

She stood stock still on her porch, looking into the face of a man who loved her so much he was crumpling before her very eyes. He'd been right there in front of her so many times over the years, in so many iterations. She'd watched him grow, ache, flourish, wither, and sprout again. He'd fallen down hard, but he'd righted himself. And, she realized with a pang, he'd righted himself for *her*. In the name of his love for her. Fearlessly. And now it was her turn. Within his eyes, she finally saw it. The moment they were sharing was the very coordination of God, the universe, and Jack, all conspiring to help write her love story, if only she would wield the pen. If only she could take that first step into the unknown.

The decision clicked into place throughout her, inside and out, like a long-aching joint finally being notched into its rightful position. The words surged upward from her aching heart, as unstoppable as if they were carried by the storm itself. It was a tempest she no longer wanted to control, even if it were possible.

"I love you, Jack." Her voice was bathed in emotion, but rang clear and true against the maelstrom around them. As she spoke, she stepped across the threshold to meet him, her arms wrapping around his neck and her mouth covering his as if she were starving and he were her sole sustenance. Their kiss was everything they'd both been yearning for, every question and affirmation they'd been holding back. It was all-consuming, a magical brew of tears, rain, and free-flowing emotion.

Jack broke the kiss to let out a gleeful sob, then pushed their bodies back under cover inside the door. Once there, he dropped to his knees at her feet, his arms clasped around her waist and his face buried in the material of her dress. She could feel his tears wetting the fabric, hear him muttering words of love in a melange of English and his own Bahamian dialect. As her hands found his rain-damp hair, his hands grasped at her legs, her waist, her buttocks, any part of her within reach, as if she could float away at any moment.

His lips roved in ardent thankfulness across her front, kissing atop her cotton shift from belly to thigh and from one hip to the other, his mouth forming her name over and over again, murmuring her into her, his voice and the rainfall a beautiful duet.

As his hands gradually began to move under the hem of her sundress to caress the softness of her haunches and the backs of her thighs, the air began to change, to charge, lightning entering their veins. Her legs parting just so; his hand lifting the hem of her dress to kiss the tender joint between her left leg and hip, the front of her panties, and the connection of her right leg and hip; his fingers moving aside the silk material, allowing his tongue to sneak into her tenderest flesh once, then twice, burning her with its delicate tasting.

Munie cried out his name and the dam broke. His hands immediately reached for the elastic strings at her waist, pulling her panties deftly down her legs and over her feet. Then, lifting her right leg over his shoulder, Jack devoured her, wantonly licking and sucking at her sex as he moaned into her, all heat and want and vibration, one hand behind her to pull her even closer to his mouth while the thumb of the opposite hand brazenly explored inside, dipping in and out and circling over and over within her in all directions.

"Jack!" Her pleading voice echoed against the night. It was too much but not enough. Not nearly enough. "I need... but we can't..."

He moved his hand from her buttocks to his pants pocket, pulling out a full strip of condoms, and gazed up at her from between her legs. "I hoped," he whispered simply.

Munie let out a cry of relief. "I need you. Now," she breathed.

Within seconds he was standing between her legs, her right leg hooked against his hip, their foreheads touching, breaths mirroring each other.

"Jack."

"Munie."

There was no more time to waste; the desperation between them was too great. His full, single thrust into her body caused them to cry out in unison, so overwhelming was the sensation. So right. So perfect. Perfection again and again as they drove their bodies together as deeply as possible, tears and kisses landing messily as they gave over control of themselves to whatever this phenomenon was. They came together in a silent cry, Munie pinned by Jack's body against the wall of her porch in front of the pouring rain.

23

[UNTITLED]

SOMETIMES NO WORDS ARE NECESSARY. WITHOUT A SINGLE ONE, JACK sent his arms under Munie's haunches to lift her against him, their bodies still connected, their eyes never leaving each other.

He fumbled his way further into the cottage, slamming the door with his foot, alternately kissing her neck and looking for the bedroom. She simply held on, allowing him to support her weight, filling her senses with the scent of him, the strong swell of his shoulders, the feel of him shifting and moving inside her as he walked. Once there, he deposited her gently on the bed, leaving her with a kiss to clean up in the bathroom. He returned with a warm, wet hand towel, and moving onto the bed beside her, placed it gently between her legs.

"I was a little rough, sorry," he whispered as he cared for her, reverently applying the towel to her softest skin and punctuating his work with tender kisses.

She had no words left nor desire to speak them, so she simply stroked his beautiful face. His hair was a mop of curls, the rain and humidity making them stand taller and fuller, spilling all over in a joyful tumble. His lips were as swollen as hers likely were from their frenzied kissing, round and full and tawny, like honey. His eyes were focused on his work until at length he sensed her watching. When they slowly made their way back home to hers, she smiled down at him.

"Come here," she whispered, pulling him onto the bed beside her and resting her head on his chest. She could feel and smell the raindrops on his tee shirt, and the gentle thud of his heartbeat was her own personal lullaby. She heard him exhale a long, slow breath. His words rumbled against her ear. "Why'd you run away?"

"Where do I start?"

"Start at the beginning."

It was good that he wasn't looking at her; it made the words easier to say.

"I knew I loved you after Nick's party, but it scared the hell out of me." She hitched a thigh across his body and snuggled in closer, feeling his arms tighten gently around her, buffeting her. "There was no closure after that—I was flying around aimless. So I came here to make peace with it all. I thought I'd see you, talk to you, figure out where to put this thing once and for all." She laughed softly and lifted her head to look at him, her chin supported in the hand resting on his chest. "But as soon as I saw you, I realized that this is bigger than me or my ability to manage it. I can't control my heart with you, Jack. And it freaked me out."

"How do you feel now?" His fingers caressed a path up and down her cheek, his touch soft as silk, his gaze gentle.

She rested her head back down on his chest. "After what just happened, it's so much deeper and bigger than it was even an hour ago. But at the same time, now I'm afraid of not having this—now that I know how incredible it feels."

She sighed long and eased off his torso to rest on her side, facing him. "Your turn. At Nick's house you said I changed you. How?"

He turned his body toward hers, kissed her gently, and began running his fingers lightly through her hair. "Before that day in Studio City, I was about to hit rock bottom. The tabloids, the using, all the stuff I had to work out, it was eating me up from the inside. Then after that day, after I found you and lost you again, everything just went further south. About a month after the interview, I hit the bottom of the seesaw hard. Real hard."

"As bad as 2015?"

He frowned, brows furrowed. "Worse. I was flat on the ground. I don't even remember some of it. Nick saved my life—got me into rehab, found me a good therapist. He took care of me."

Munie was speechless, so she just stroked his face.

"When I got clean, your words came back to me. But this time I really heard them. And they gave me life. You gave me a window to see another version of myself. A real one." He pushed upward onto an elbow, resting his head in his hand. "I started dreaming, Munie. I started believing. It was a fucking incredible feeling. Then COVID hit, and I had no reason not to hunker down and really go for it."

She was almost too moved to speak, but her heart was too close to bursting to not let her next words come out. "I'm proud of you, Jack."

He kissed her softly. "Your turn. Do you believe me?"

"About remembering?" She paused, searching within herself. "Yes. But why didn't you recognize me back then? It hurt me deeply, Jack."

He kissed her forehead and sighed. "I know, and I'm so, so sorry. It's something the therapist and I worked on for a long time." He paused, as if struggling for words.

"You don't have to talk about it if you're not ready."

His response was immediate. "There's nothing I don't want to share with you, Munie." He sat up in the bed and stroked her face. "At first, I couldn't figure it out—why I remembered Via Clara but nothing else. I beat myself up about that for over a year after Studio City. When I tell you it landed in me like a bullet, that's exactly how it felt." He sighed long. "As soon as you mentioned LA and New York, all that time came flooding back—all the sweet moments, all the... damn... all the intimate moments—and all of a sudden I was the biggest asshole in the world."

She sat up as well so that they were eye to eye. "It sounds like a block. You didn't remember, but then as soon as I mentioned it, poof! It was all right there."

"Yeah." Jack rubbed a hand down his face, causing Munie to pre-empt his next words with a kiss. "That's what the therapist and I talked about. She said there was a trigger, and I guess for me it was when you left Via Clara that day and didn't come back. It hurt me, so I built a wall." He took her hand, intertwining their fingers. "I'm not sure what you call it scientifically or anything, but for a long time I basically closed myself off to anything that would get under my skin—anything that could hit my heart."

"Like a defense mechanism."

"Yeah. I guess I blocked out anything deep."

"Maybe that's why you could remember those women in the songs—a night dancing on the beach and a one-night stand in Singapore? Because they were more... casual?"

"Exactly! But when it came to you, I blocked you out, because somewhere deep, I knew that if I recognized you, I'd remember getting hurt."

"Oh Jack..." She looked down, crestfallen. "Now *I* feel like the biggest asshole in the world."

"Baby, look at me." He lifted her chin with his hand to look at her with smiling eyes. "You undid all that too, that day in Studio City. You told me to feel whatever was inside, to get naked, right? And I had to. So I did it—I'm on the other side now. And I owe all that to you." With that, he sent his hand behind her head and kissed her long on the mouth.

When he pulled back, his eyes searched hers for a long time, his expression tied up in a flurry of emotions. "Now I'm returning the favor. Munie, I need to ask you to do something."

"What?"

"Take the leap with me. Trust that I will hold your heart in my hands every day, that you can give it to me and know it's safe. Just step off the diving board. That's all I ask. Don't try to control it. Just let it take you. Can you do that?"

She looked deeply into his open, seeking eyes. He'd jumped off already with both feet, changing everything for the better, for her. It was her turn.

"Just keep holding my hand?"

He let out a choked breath as his eyes filled with tears, and he made no pretense of hiding them. He brought her hand to his lips and kissed it tenderly, then placed it against his chest. "Woman, I want nothing more than to hold this hand every day for the rest of my life. I love you so much, Munie. And I got you. Always."

She smiled through her own tears, and whispered, "OK then. Let's go."

He was hers. From his shining eyes to his beautiful mind to the heart beating with love for her, he was hers. The urge to see all of him came over her in a gentle wave. She stood, taking his hand and guiding him to stand facing her.

Lifting his tee shirt one inch at a time slowly revealed his torso; she kissed each inch of skin as it came into view. Her gaze fell to the tattoo over his heart, registering a difference in the image from the version etched in her memory. Below the original music staff was a series of characters. With a gasp, she realized it was her Sanskrit name—Rai—the lettering delicate and perfectly rendered. When she looked back up at him, dumbfounded, he just smiled gently. She let her lips graze over the wording, kissing the intention as well as the action, and then pushed the fabric further upward, Jack helping to pull it overhead and off. She stepped back to take in the radiance of his naked torso, her eyes traveling over well-formed shoulders and muscular arms. His chest was just as smooth and broad as she remembered, with skin the color of almonds and nipples a bit darker in contrast. She tasted them one at a time, and was rewarded with his sharp intake of breath. Jack.

One button, one zip, and the loose linen pants were pooled at his feet. Her hands inside his boxers, one on each of his strong hips, and with a gentle push, they quickly joined the pile. Without looking down, Munie melted into his embrace, letting her body revel in the feel of his warm skin from tip to toes, her hands slowly exploring, re-acquainting themselves with the contours of his body.

Jack stepped back after a few moments, smiling broadly for the first time since he'd appeared at her door. He crouched in front of her, his palms flush against the outside of her knees, and moved upward until he caught hold of her dress, lifting it overhead and off in one motion. But then his smile disappeared, and tears filled his eyes once again.

"My God, Munie." He stared at her silently for several seconds, spellbound and reverent. She found she couldn't breathe for want of his touch. Finally, one tentative finger reached out to trace her right collarbone, slowly following a path toward her sternum and down between her breasts. He gazed in wonderment as his fingers moved to feel the contours of her right breast, exploring the little raised dots of her areola and the firm pop of her nipple. She let out a little moan of pleasure, and he took her into his mouth, lifting her again to carry them both to bed.

It was as if he was attempting to memorize every detail of her body, so rapt was he as he kissed his way across her torso, her arms, shoulders and belly, savoring all the tender places hidden around her. And she caught fire as he went, reeling in the familiar yet new sensation of his soft mouth inside her elbow, between her fingers, at her navel. It was almost more than she could bear. He was tortuously slow, tortuously skilled, as if she were an instrument under his hands and mouth, being strummed to perfection.

By the time his mouth reached the apex between her legs, she was crazy with want, but still he was slow, teasingly deliberate, tasting her inside and out. Jack Flores knew exactly how to please a woman, and unlike last time, was not so lost in her that he couldn't apply those skills, nipping here, licking there, finding rhythms and angles that made her writhe under him. And each time he stopped or changed position, he would smile that sly, devilish grin before dipping his head to make her cry out again from a new but just as intense sensation.

The rain poured down in sheets, the ocean waves roared in the wind, and Munie found her shattering release with Jack's tongue deep within her, his moans of pleasure singing their way through her body from the inside. He took his time as she came down, savoring every drop of her as his hands stroked her thighs, her backside, the tender skin at the inside of her hip joint. He kept up his slow torment until he felt her begin to quicken again, and only then did he start the journey back up her body in the same slow motion, rolling upward with kisses until his form was flush against hers, his lips at her ear.

"I want to tattoo myself into you so that you feel me every minute of every day." His first movement was tentative, his eyes locked on hers as he eased inside, taking in every note on her face. With his body, he responded to her smallest intake of breath, the most minute change in her expression, altering angle and pressure and rhythm to fit the song she was singing for him, a maestro bringing out her aria. He wrote her melody artfully, over and over again, taking his time and ultimately penning his own crescendo with and within her.

24

LET'S STAY TOGETHER

"WHY CAN'T I STOP TOUCHING YOU?"

Jack marveled at the phenomenon even as his fingers continued to skim lazily over Munie's skin, taking in all her contours and textures. It was true; even with their passion temporarily sated, they'd spent the last two hours in bed just kissing, caressing, and napping, their bodies wrapped around each other.

"I don't think we're supposed to stop," was her only response as she sleepily sampled his love-swollen lips. Devoid of cologne, fancy mouthwash, and other trappings, Jack tasted just like a gingerbread cookie. And Munie loved gingerbread. And with no commitments, there was no reason not to stay here all day enjoying his marvelous flavor ...

Suddenly, she ended the kiss to pull back and look at him with wide eyes.

"You missed your party!" He simply raised a quizzical eyebrow in response, and bent his head to nuzzle under her ear, but she leaned away, tapping him on the shoulder for emphasis.

"Your reception! After the show last night. You got here around midnight, which means you missed your own party."

He just gazed at her, smiling. "Baby, you still aren't getting it, are you? None of that matters worth a fuck to me anymore. To hell with the parties, to hell with the press, to hell with all the expectations and appearances and all the rest of it." He kissed her softly. "Being there for my kids, making music that means something, and you. That's my life now. I'm yours, Munie. One thousand percent."

He watched her closely, waiting for his words to truly sink in. When they did, she just melted against him and sighed, their bodies inextricably entwined under the light cotton sheets.

She woke to the smell of coffee and the unmistakable sizzle of a skillet at work. Sure enough, when she padded out to the kitchen wearing Jack's hopelessly wrinkled linen shirt, she found him at the stove in his boxers, a tea towel slung over his bare shoulder and a spatula in his hand, singing along to some station or other on the cottage's smart speaker. It was a sight she wanted to see every single day for the rest of her life.

"Mornin.'" Ah, the dimples were awake too, apparently. She couldn't resist kissing the mouth between them, a connection that went deeper and longer than she had originally anticipated.

"Smells wonderful."

"I figure we'll need the energy if I'm going to make love to you all afternoon," he crooned into her ear. Abandoning the stove, he wrapped his arms around her and planted an open-mouthed kiss on the side of her neck, sighing into her ear as he tasted her skin. "As much as I'd love to just feast on you right now." He kissed her long and slow, pressing her body against the counter. If she were to reply, it would be with a comeback that laid bare the level of heat already building back up within her.

As if to ensure a meal would indeed happen, the skillet suddenly let out a nefarious hiss, compelling Jack to release her from his embrace and take up his spatula once again.

"You'd better focus, Iron Chef." She hopped onto the bar stool opposite him, gratefully accepting the cup of coffee that he poured out for her with his non-stirring hand. Her eyes closed, she inhaled its rich aroma and sighed long in satisfaction. "Mmmmm." She felt deep contentment just sitting there, silently sipping and watching the beautiful form of the man she loved move nimbly about the small kitchen.

He was a tidily messy cook, she noted. There were open containers all over the counter, but no crumbs, spills, or other debris to be found. She spotted a wooden cutting board covered with the herbs she'd bought at the market earlier in the week, a carton bearing the shells of her six remaining eggs, and the open Tupperware container of sautéed kale and tomatoes from dinner two nights ago. Impressive. He even tossed around that tea towel with the aplomb of a cooking show contestant.

"What?" He caught her watching, and grinned.

"You're really enjoying yourself, aren't you?"

"Absolutely." With legitimate flair, he flipped the omelet in midair, caught it deftly back in the pan, and returned it to the burner.

She rolled her eyes and laughed. "Showoff."

"That's me." He plated the food, even adding a few leftover salad greens for color, and slid the dishes over to Munie's side of the counter.

"Thank you. This looks fantastic."

"Anytime." He walked around the kitchen island to take a seat beside her, kissing her on the cheek. "Dig in."

They were silent for a few ravenous minutes, precisely as two hungry foodies should be, the quiet accentuated only by the clink of their forks, the clunk of their mugs on the counter, and their occasional groans of culinary bliss.

After a few moments of this quaint rhythm, he looked out the window to the ocean beyond and sighed. "I like it here."

Munie straightened up in her seat and turned to face him, brows furrowed. "How the hell did you find me, anyway?"

He laughed a little sheepishly, gazing back at her from over his coffee mug, mischief making his brown eyes twinkle.

"After I saw you in the crowd, I went to Micah before the encore—"

"During the show?!"

"Yeah. I knew you two were friends, but he said he had no idea where you were staying. He also looked at me like I had three heads."

"Ha! I can only imagine."

"And I was desperate." He put down the cup to focus on his words, on her. "Munie, you have no idea. I saw your face, looking like that, crying like that, and then I watched you rush away, and my whole heart just dropped right out of my body." She took his hand in hers, and he drew a deep, long breath. "The absolute only option in my head was that, in the interview, you mentioned that somebody named Glenys was your best friend—"

"What?!"

"And that was the last arrow I had left. So I asked Micah if he knew her."

Her eyes would not budge from their fish-like stare—she could virtually feel her eyebrows touching the ceiling. "No you didn't! What did he say?"

"He opened his mouth like a carp and turned about eight different colors." Munie had of course just taken a sip of coffee, and it took everything she had not to spit it all over her companion. "Girl, it took me fifteen solid minutes after the show to get through to that man. He really loves you, you know."

She smiled, looking down. "I know. I'm lucky." She looked back up, her eyes still wide as saucers. "What did you say to him?"

Jack ran his fingers down the sides of his mouth, thinking. "I honestly don't remember. But let's just say this—he now has absolutely no doubt that I am completely and utterly in love with you. So he finally gave me Glenys' number."

She put down her mug to stare at him more effectively. "You called Glenys???"

"Hell yes. I called six times and she didn't pick up."

"She wouldn't, if she didn't know who was calling."

"Right. So I tracked down Micah again and had him text her."

"And?" Munie was completely engrossed and fascinated.

"Her ass called *me*."

"No!"

"Yep. Then I spent another twenty minutes telling your best friend how much I loved you before she'd dish on where you were. She had me crying and everything."

"Oh Jack … she didn't tell me … why didn't she text me?" Munie looked out the window, bewildered, then felt Jack's soft touch at her chin, inviting her to look at him.

"I asked her to tell you. She said no, because she wasn't going to, in her words, 'piss on the most magical moment of your life.'"

Munie was too moved to speak, so she just stared at him. She watched as a grin slowly unfurled across his face. "And then she said that if I hurt a single hair on your head or fucked around with your heart, she would, also in her words, 'rip off my dick and feed it to me.'"

At this, Munie burst out in gut-deep laughter, which made Jack do the same. They bellowed until tears rolled down their faces. It felt like a release valve cranking open to let out all the drama and tension of the past twenty four hours.

Jack was prone to fits of giggles, and once he'd started, it was a long-term investment. And so, each time their laughter began to die down, his high-pitched, slightly airy giggle would burst across them again, sending Munie right back into hysterics.

"Sometimes," she finally managed to choke out, "Glen changes the script and adds a drink."

"What?" he squeaked.

"Uh huh. We went to Vegas for her birthday a few years ago, and the hotel lost the bag she left at bag check." Munie took a swig of coffee and a deep breath in order to get the next sentence out. "The bellman said something really rude to her—I don't even remember what—and she told him that if he didn't comb the back room and find her luggage, she'd feed him his dick with a double shot of Laphroig to wash it down with!"

Jack howled, tipping off balance and almost falling off his stool. "Oh shit. I can't wait to meet her, man," he cackled, wiping his eyes on the tea towel.

Thoughts of reality suddenly came crashing down on Munie,

bringing her back to Earth and instantly altering her expression from merry to sober.

"Jack?"

"Yeah, baby?" he asked hoarsely, a silly grin still on his face. Looking over at her, it immediately morphed into a mirror image of the mask she was wearing. "What's wrong? Tell me."

She looked around the space of the cottage, then cast her eyes out the window to the calm, post-storm sea, all part of the safe haven of love in which they were resting.

"What happens next?" It came out in a whisper, the overpowering sensation of loss pressing like a vise against her throat.

"Munie." His voice was gentle.

"I'm serious. We both have to leave here sometime, we both have lives to live. When do you fly out?"

Jack looked down at his hands, dejection written all over his face. "Tomorrow. I'm flying to St Louis for Zenith's birthday."

Silence echoed across the room in stark contrast with the laughter of a few minutes before. Munie and Jack could almost hear the other grappling with the reality that their just-built bubble of protection would soon be washed away like words in the sand, leaving no trace of its existence. At length, it was Jack who dipped a toe back in the water.

"I know it's a lot. If it's not something you can sign up for, I get it."

"What?" Munie looked at him with knitted brows bordering sad, sad eyes.

"I come with a soccer team, like you said. They all live with their moms, but they're a big part of my life now. I know you said you never wanted kids, and—"

"Jack, do you remember everything I said in that interview?" she interjected, stunned.

"Every word. And not just the interview." He reached out to stroke her cheek. "If all of that isn't what you wanted to sign up for, I get it. I really do."

She looked into his eyes, guileless, open, and just as vulnerable as she felt. "Is that what you're afraid of?" He didn't reply, but simply continued to gaze at her, taking in every inch of her face. "Jack, I want all of you. I love everything that comes with you, and it would be an honor for me to know your children."

She watched as his face transformed, relief and joy washing over him and brimming over in his eyes as tears.

"Are you serious?"

In response, she brought her hands to each side of his face, bringing him close. "Of course, Jack. I'm all in."

He pulled her into his full embrace so that she sat astride him on his stool, the better to hold her to him and kiss her.

"What else is holding you back?" he breathed between kisses, his hands roving across her skin under his linen shirt.

"Nothing. But what about you?" Her hands were tangled in his curls, her mouth tasting him more urgently and deeply by the second.

"Absolutely nothing."

They both stopped cold, staring at each other, awareness dawning like a new morning between them.

"Then that's it," he whispered, wonder coloring his tone. "It's us. Forever."

She nodded, eyes locked onto his, her joy mirroring his own. All of a sudden, he rose from his seat, placed her feet gently on the floor, and held out his hand to her, eyes shining.

"Munie Paley, will you dance with me?"

"Always," she breathed as she took his hand and snuggled into his embrace. Munie and Jack held onto each other, their gazes locked as they swayed slowly to the gentle rhythm of the waves outside the window, The Reverend Al Green's 'Let's Stay Together' playing in the background.

SONGS **on this Track**

Let's Stay Together: Songwriters Al Green, Willie Mitchell, Al Jackson Jr.; performed by the Reverend Al Green

25

BONUS TRACK

June 2029
Via Clara, CA

"That could easily have been the best breakfast I've ever had—even better than a Full Scottish." The two friends were walking arm-in-arm down the sidewalk—inner elbows linked, outer hands clutching to-go cups of some of the best coffee either could remember having had in recent years. Munie sipped slowly, savoring the notes of chocolate and cherry on her tongue.

"I can see why you've picked Via Clara," Glenys continued. "It's absolutely charming." Munie took in the familiar storefronts and the newer green space with fresh eyes, attempting to see it again for the first time, as her friend was doing now. "Much more wholesome than the swamp."

Munie laughed. "The perks of being a documentary writer, I suppose. Swamp visits by choice only. And to be honest, with all the refurbishment work here over the last few months, I haven't been back to L.A. in a long time."

"And Jack?"

She took another sip and sighed in contentment. "Same. He loves being out of the city. That's why he built the studio on the second floor. They were going to sell the whole property and turn it into some highbrow clothing store. He swooped in literally three days before the sale was final and bought both units."

"Well-played, indeed. But does no one come in pestering him for autographs?"

"Not really, but just in case, we had a separate studio entrance built in the back, complete with security code."

"Brilliant as usual, ducks."

"Why thank you!" Munie pointed in front of her. "Here—this is it. You're really going to love it, Glen."

They had come to a stop in front of *Ray's Place*, a retro-style storefront visibly undisturbed by the slow gentrification around it, aside from fresh landscaping and the gleam of a new paint job. Munie held open the door for Glenys and then passed through behind her, the bell over the entryway heralding them a cheerful welcome home.

"Blimey, I haven't seen vinyl in a hundred years!" Glenys gave a little giggle as she looked around at the neat record bins, the wall hangings, and the just-right retro decor. It smelled like a heady combination of old records and new flooring, with some incense thrown in there for good measure. A young employee at a desk in the corner waved them hello with a smile. They waved back, and Glenys headed off to the right to begin browsing as Munie passed down the opposite aisle.

Munie let her fingers caress the covers one by one, blissfully losing all track of time, until she heard Glenys emit a small screech from her station halfway across the room. Turning her head toward the sound, Munie watched her walk toward the desk while tapping pointedly at the album cover in her hand.

"What in the actual fuck? Can you explain this to me, please?"

"Sorry ma'am—how can I help?"

"You can't seriously tell me that bizarre shite like this is actually for sale?"

"It is."

"It's a legitimate work?"

"One hundred percent."

"And it's available for purchase?"

"Yes ma'am."

Munie, now perfectly intrigued, caught a glimpse of the front cover as Glenys flipped over the jacket to examine the back. She found herself looking at the image of a man in a cowboy hat, the words *Country Bar Mitzvah* written above it somewhere in the title. She stifled a guffaw as Glenys looked back up at the young man, her eyes wide with merriment. "How much?"

From her vantage point, Munie could see him begin to laugh as well, his shoulders shaking gently. "Come on over to the register. We can work something out."

"Thank you...?"

"Zenith," he replied, extending his hand. "Zenith Kensington."

Glenys smiled broadly, taking his hand in both of hers and shaking it aerobically. "Ah brilliant, Zenith. I'm Glenys. So lovely to finally meet you."

Still smiling, Munie continued to flip through the familiar contents of the jazz section... Herb Alpert, Miles Davis, Oscar Peterson. The next item in the stack was new to her eyes—*Canciones de Amor*, by Esai Morales. She picked it up to examine it as footsteps approached beside her, a low, seductive voice flowing like a tonic into her ear.

"I've got a signed version of that in the back room, if you'd like to check it out. That's where we keep all the really good stuff."

Raising her gaze from the cover in her hand, she took in the always-appealing view of Jack, cutting a lean profile in jeans and a black v-neck sweater, a pair of reading glasses just barely visible above a mass of tight salt-and-pepper curls. His smile spread into a pair of slightly naughty dimples; she kissed the mouth between them tenderly.

He peeked over to see what she was looking at. "Hey, you found it. I just got three copies from my cousin Manolo. I think they only cut, like, a hundred, so I'm stoked I got them. Check it out."

He took the cover from her hand and turned it over to show her the group image on the back. Eight musicians in tuxedos smiled back at her. She let her gaze rove down the line of faces but stopped short at the end, awareness blooming in her heart. A young, earnest Jack... Jackson... smiled proudly into the camera. Somewhere in the deepest part of her heart, the circle came complete with a subtle click.

Munie looked from the young man in the photo back up to her husband, the same joyful, young soul in a fully-grownup body. She smiled at him with all the love in the world. "I'd love to see more of the good stuff."

He grinned back at her, eyes and dimples shining. "Let's go."

ACKNOWLEDGMENTS

Well, I suppose I should first thank my therapist, Gaynor.

It was her suggestion that started this whole book in motion, after all. During one of our weekly sessions, she mentioned it might be helpful for me to start journaling. I gamely replied, "Absolutely not. I loathe journaling." It's not like I haven't tried—I'm a certified health and wellness coach and a yoga instructor, and concepts like journaling in those circles are as *en vogue* as the now-ubiquitous oat milk latte.

However, I was determined to stand my ground on this one, and she was just as determined to figure out some kind of outlet for me. "Doodling?" Nah. "A photo diary?" Nope—too much like journaling, and I have waaaaay too many photos in my iPhone to be sorting through them as a wellness activity. A glimmer in her eye, she came to the plate one more time. "Free writing?" she offered.

Six months and 50,000 words later, Jack and Munie exist. The scenes just fell out of my head somehow. They were right there, in three dimensions and living color, and all I had to do was get them on paper. I drafted in a notebook first (OK, a "journal"), which I think was a huge help in drawing the characters' unique shapes, and then I simply colored them in on the laptop. I have to thank Gaynor for that a-ha moment—until now I've only written on iPhone and computer. But I do believe, in this case, the literal application of "pen to paper" helped me both mentally and creatively.

My next enormous swell of thanks goes to "the Amys." First is my high school bestie, Amy Helt (she goes by Mel in some of my lifestyle blogs). I'm ridiculously private about being a creative writer, and she is one of the very, very few people who actually know about this aspect of me. She's been wonderfully supportive, discreet, and an immensely helpful beta reader. She is my cheerleader, my happy place, and a hellion with punctuation and syntax. Who could ask for more?

The other Amy in this phenomenal pair is my editor, Amy Ewing. Oh gosh, where do I even begin? Let me just say this. Burgeoning writers can really be low in self-confidence, and this is a tough, tough space. From the moment she said she loved my sample and wanted to edit it, her unwavering support has literally kept me writing. I wouldn't have had the *chutzpah* to put this book out there if it weren't for her. And let's get down to brass tacks—without her brilliant suggestions at the developmental stage, which, in the parlance of Spinal Tap, took things "to eleven," *Studio City Songs* wouldn't be nearly what it is today. Her suggestions opened Pandora's box to a host of additional content, linkages and connection points that didn't exist, but needed to. The love story between Munie and Jack now feels complete, and Amy Ewing, it's all your fault! :) I thank you endlessly.

My next kudos are for graphic artist Julia DeCamp, who gamely took on a draft cover in her free time, and proceeded to blow my mind with what she created. I wanted so much to convey both the musicality and the romance of the piece—she did that just perfectly, and then some. See you again for the next book, Julia!

I'm not a musician, but I'm a giant music fan. *Studio City Songs* has a strong musical backbeat, and I'd be remiss if I didn't call out some of the artists who lent their inspiration to its pages. Hats off to (in alpha order) Adele, Sebastian Bach, Count Basie, Tony Bennett, Bobby Caldwell, John Coltrane, Sam Cooke, Celia Cruz, Miles Davis, Dr. Nathan Davis, El DeBarge, Duke Ellington, Cynthia Erivo, Ella Fitzgerald, Aretha Franklin, Marvin Gaye, Astrud Gilberto, Billie Holiday, Quincy Jones, John Lennon, Barry Manilow, Bruno Mars, George Michael, Joni Mitchell, Prince, Tito Puente, Frank Sinatra, Grover Washington, Jr. and a whole slew of other geniuses whose work simmered in my brain while I wrote.

A book is nothing without its reader. Thank you for reading these pages and listening to the love song of Jack and Munie. I hope you enjoyed getting to know them as much as I enjoyed writing them.

Finally, and always in the forefront of my heart, all my love and thanks to my guys. You know who you are. You keep my world turning. You are my moon.

With much love,

Zaide

ABOUT THE AUTHOR

Zaide Williams is a fiction and nonfiction writer, yoga teacher, wellness coach, and occasional corporate suit. She lives outside Atlanta, GA with her husband, son and multiple beasts. A giant foodie with an appetite for travel, she also loves a good concert, and her favorite artists are her son on piano and husband on guitar. Learn more about her and her work at zaidewilliams.com.

BONUS CONTENT
PORTRAIT OF THE WANDERER:

An Interview with Gene Coltrane
By Rai Paley
January 2020

We've seen many iterations of Gene Coltrane over the last 15 years, from earnest boy next door to jazz prodigy to R&B hustler to writer and producer extraordinaire. His story is the stuff of fairy tales—a boy with immense musical talent, brought up in a working-class family of professional musicians and blessed with a fairy sprinkle of good looks and a clever mind, all pulling together to create a prolific artist with a legendary work ethic and unforgettable charisma. But who is the man at the center of this nested set of gifts?

I didn't know which Gene I'd find when I sat down to talk with him about his life and projects thus far. He is famously reluctant to be interviewed about anything other than his music, so I was intrigued as to how much access I would get to the man behind the larger-than-life persona.

What greeted me when I entered the room was a study in contrasts. A designer suit jacket, Gap tee shirt, and a few gold chains.

Store-brand jeans, highly-polished shoes and $500 sunglasses. Hair naturally shaped into a dense, close-cropped Afro. A Rolex watch and a simple, woven cotton bracelet donning his wrist. Dimples and that understandably famous smile joining forces to welcome me, along with a cottony, tropical scent, as if he had just bathed under a waterfall in Maui. Maybe he had.

The man awaiting me exemplified charm and put-together ease. But when I took my seat opposite him, I noticed that there were faint lines outside that dimpled grin, which went as far as his sunglasses but gave no further story. And as I got closer, I detected—just subtly under that tropical fragrance—the faint staleness of a recently snuffed-out cigarette.

It's been a challenging few years for the artist. On one hand, his latest album, *Blue Sky*, is a resounding success with music critics and the general listening population alike, with Grammy buzz in the air not just for Jazz Album of the Year, but overall Album of the Year and Songwriter of the Year as well. Tours are selling out quickly, and collaboration opportunities—of which Coltrane is well-known to be fond—are flying toward him from all directions.

But it's the other side of fame that's been wearisome this year in particular. Gene Coltrane has always been known as both a music man and a ladies' man. Since his first rise to the charts, the tabloids have been ruthless in their charting of his relationships, break-ups and extracurricular dalliances. When rumor began this past April regarding his alleged fathering of two children with different fans in different cities, the buzz overtook the narrative, relegating the brilliance of his fourth album to a footnote in the entertainment news.

But Coltrane is ready now to set the record straight. He is the father of four children, ranging in age from ten to two and residing in different locations around the world. While he will not offer any further details regarding the children or their mothers—non-celebrities all—in consideration for the privacy of everyone involved, he did have the following to share with me on the topic:

"I'm mortal, you know? I'm passionate. And sometimes I let that emotion take over. When I write, it makes for a great song. But in life, it makes for some 'heat of the moment' decisions that have longer-term consequences for people other than me. I guess I just like to be in love."

Even given the complexity of circumstance, however, Coltrane—who came from a large family himself—is finding joy in the concept of fatherhood. He is supporting each of his children and their mothers financially, and tries his hardest to spend quality time with them as much as his lifestyle of almost constant travel allows. "I get this gift," he said, "and I don't want to mess it up. I want to be there ... not just on paper, but really be there. Really be a father."

Substance abuse has also formed a part of Coltrane's story. I was surprised to learn that he had been very close to the late trombonist Lark Benson, who tragically died from a heroin overdose in 2008. The two had even been roommates early in their careers, sharing a small space in Via Clara, CA from 2003 to 2007, when Coltrane signed with *Theta Records* and his star began to rise.

Coltrane himself was arrested for possession in 2015. While it would be easy to veer off the deep end of this topic, our conversation focused instead on the music that came from this time. Following his arrest, the artist went into a seclusion of sorts, cordoning himself off from the world in his home and studio. Brilliance followed, to include the entire *Blue Sky* album as well as now chart-topping collaborations with artists such as Nickles Boone, with whom he's worked several times over the years, rapper Donnie Prince, and ingenue Tiyani Keith, all completed within the space of six months—brilliance in a bottle.

It is precisely this phenomenon that fans want to understand. What comes next for this gifted musician, who recalls the time it takes to write masterpieces like "Green" in hours versus weeks or months? What is in the mind of the producer who pulls greatness from artists as disparate as P.O. and Tiyani Keith? What might we expect to hear from the man whose vocal gifts perhaps even surpass his skill as an instrumentalist? Who is Gene Coltrane, truly?

Only he knows the answer to that question. Only Coltrane himself can select among the entities within him to bring out the truest and purest version of himself for the world to see. And if, as I suspect, my own sentiments reflect those of the greater audience, the world will be waiting with open arms.